CAMP OF THE SAINTS

CAMP OF THE SAINTS

A NOVEL

BRAD E HAINSWORTH

ISBN: 1-55517-150-8
Library of Congress
Catalog Card Number: 94-72280

Published and Distributed by:

CFI
Cedar Fort, Incorporated
925 North Main, Springville, UT 84663   801-489-4084

Cover design by Lyle Mortimer
Page layout and design by Brian L. Carter
Printed in the United States of America

DEDICATION

For Justin, Travis, Tyler, Megan, and Caitlynn.
And for all those little souls yet to come.

Author's Note

This book is a work of fiction and what might be thought of as approximate history. It is based on a great deal of careful research and analysis, and though many events described herein did take place, and though many historical figures appear in its pages, it is nonetheless a work of fiction based on historical circumstance.

Great effort has been taken to portray actual historical figures, and a good many events, as the best historical sources would lead a reasonable person to conclude they might actually have been. But, of course, for those who have encountered the mountain man, Jasper Pughsey, the only thing that can be said of him is that, as always, he is true to his own cantankerous character.

So, if the following story is not how it was, then this is how it should have been.

Brad E Hainsworth
Orem, Utah
So many years later, 1994

CHAPTER ONE

The horse's hoofs beat a hollow drum roll as Obediah Jones led the big animal off the crowded flat-boat and onto the muddy western shore of the Missouri River. The busy bank was soft from the demanding river, swollen from the melting snows of the high plains and mountains far to the west, and man and animal alike had beaten the once grassy earth into a foul-smelling waste of muck.

It had been a long, exhausting trip up the river from St. Louis where the mountain man had spent an interminably boring winter. Filled with stories over the years of the endless pleasures to be found in that restless and unruly city, he had found nothing of value. Now he longed for the open prairie, but he had especially missed the mountains—the mountains, where a man could stand in one spot and see almost to the end of the earth. Vistas so unbelievably beautiful, he could stare in one direction all day and never grow weary of the sight.

Eager to be on the move, Obediah Jones swung into the saddle, gently nudged the big horse with his heels, and cantered up the rutted wagon trail away from the busy river toward Fort Leavenworth, Kansas Territory—bleeding Kansas, caught up in the fury of states' rights and slavery.

The government reservation spread west from the top of the bluffs overlooking the river out onto the plains. Leavenworth served as the trailhead for both the Oregon and Santa Fe Trails, a rude, bustling hive of activity filled with the human flotsam of the turbulent westward expansion.

Obediah Jones reached the crest of the bluff and spurred his horse at a faster pace along Kearney Avenue to the entrance of the Leavenworth compound that sprawled along the north side of the restless thoroughfare. He turned through the front gate and reined up in front of the Quarter Master's building. The long frame building fronted onto the post's parade ground which was crowded with wagons being loaded with large quantities of supplies. Troops, teamsters, hired hands, and roustabouts of almost every description were sweating in the heat of the spring afternoon as they labored to fill each wagon. Obediah dismounted and stood watching the men as they worked at what seemed a frantic pace.

"Well, I'll be confounded...if it ain't Obediah Jones."

Obediah was not pleased to see the squat, slovenly trapper who was standing with several other men in the shade of the building's covered porch. "Well, as I live and breathe, if it isn't Benko Tatum," Obediah mockingly replied. "The last I saw of you was your backside disappearing into the trees barely ahead of some mighty upset Sioux. I thought your scalp'd be hanging on some happy warrior's lodge a long time ago, though I don't know how they'd pull it off."

"Now, now...ain't like it was, ya know," the man said, spitting a stream of black tobacco juice into the corner of the porch. "Good times'r gone, now, Obediah. No beaver t' make the dangers worth the while. Settlers'r movin' west almost in hordes." A muddy gob of spittle hung from his hairless chin.

The most remarkable thing about Benko Tatum was his eyes. He had the eyes of a snake. They never blinked. And they were set too close together, separated by a thin, short nose that was almost lost on a face too broad for its uneven features, and set in a skull that was nearly devoid of hair. When his eyes focused on a man, they never seemed to let go, holding fast on their prey. Like a snake, Tatum was a predator, always intent on his own insatiable appetites, a threat to anything and everything around him.

Tatum's eyes were focused on Obediah Jones, and Jones disliked the man intensely, viscerally. And he reacted as most men do to a snake, with the urge to stomp it to death.

"Uh-huh," Obediah said, trying not to show his complete contempt. "As I recall, it wasn't beaver those bucks were upset about. You and that vermin you travel with," he said, nodding toward the other men, "nearly got us all killed."

The assault of Tatum and his companions on the two, young Sioux women that crisp, fall day had nearly cost Obediah Jones and Jasper Pughsey their lives. The two mountain men had spent several relatively luckless weeks trapping a small stream that meandered through a lush meadow, surrounded by dense stands of Lodgepole pine and the steep, thickly forested, and brush-covered slopes of the Absaroka Mountains. Only occasionally was the vegetation broken by precipitous, unstable talus slopes leading to the cliffs that towered above.

Obediah and Jasper had been gathering their traps at a point where the stream widened out of a narrow canyon several miles from where it fed into the Yellowstone. Each morning the deep pools in the meadow were icing over, and the winter snows were not far off. To make things worse, a small party of Sioux had made an encampment not far down stream, and the situation was getting uncomfortable.

An uneasy truce had been established after the two trappers had parted with some salt and a large Green River knife one of the warriors had taken a liking to, but the two were anxious to move on, perhaps saving their scalps in the long run.

Both Obediah and Jasper had heard the shot and the women's shrill voices, but thought at first that it was nothing more than a loud dispute over some camp difficulty. Best to mind one's own business, but when the distant noise turned to distinct screams echoing up the canyon, both men grabbed their Hawkens and, staying well within the tree line, hurried toward the Sioux encampment.

Benko Tatum had shot an old Indian who had tried to protect one of the young women. The elderly redskin lay sprawled on the ground, and one of Tatum's men stood with his foot on the ancient one's bloody, gray head, threatening the camp with his rifle. Tatum and several of his men were dragging two, young Sioux women into the trees at the rear of the camp while four others herded squaws and children into two nearby tepees. Apparently off on a hunt, no Sioux men could be seen in the camp, except for a few too old or too young to be of help.

Jasper Pughsey's shot hit the man standing over the old Indian, knocking him violently to the ground, just as eight or ten mounted Sioux warriors erupted from the tree line on the down-stream side of the camp. The women and children broke and scattered as a volley of arrows caught their surprised captors. Two of Tatum's men had died in their tracks while the third ran after Tatum and the others who had disappeared into the trees where their horses were hidden. The fourth struggled to follow, an arrow buried in his chest, but was soon lost in a bloody melee as frenzied

Sioux warriors swarmed around him. One Brave gave a cruel scream as he jumped from his horse and, in a storm of dust and hooves, savagely jerked the man's scalp free with a distinct snap and waved it in the dusty air.

Almost before the echoes from Jasper's shot had died, he and Obediah had turned and run for their small camp. Both knew the enraged Sioux would not rest until the scalp of every mountain man they could find hung from their lances. Obediah and Jasper barely had time to grab some of their possibles and run for their horses before screams of the rapidly approaching warriors could be clearly heard.

"We ain't gonna make it," Jasper had yelled, his breath coming in short desperate gasps.

"Not this way...leave the horses and run...we...."

"Well now...seems you ain't all that happy I'm still numbered amongst the livin'," Tatum said, as he stepped off the porch, his unwelcome voice jerking Obediah back to the present.

"Well," Obediah said, moving away from his horse, "I guess some things just never change."

"Speakin' of which, where's that coon what was always trailin' you around?" The man spat a wad at Obediah's feet.

Obediah felt his neck redden, but kept his voice cool. "Don't know. I haven't seen Jasper in several years. Last I heard he was still out in the Rockies, somewhere around the Mormon settlements."

"Well, now, why don't that surprise me none? Seems like he always did find some trash t' pick up with an' keep 'is winters warm."

"Let me tell you something, Tatum. If...."

"'Cept I heard the dumb pork eater got hisself kilt a year 'r two ago," Tatum said, moving closer to Jones.

Obediah froze. "What exactly did you hear, Benko? And careful how you tell it."

"He got what 'e had comin'. I jest wish I'd given it to 'im," the man said, with bitterness. "But since 'e ain't here, maybe I'll jest have t' administer it t' you." Benko's knife darted into his hand from some hidden place, the movement so fast, Obediah hardly saw it. "Seems like the last time we all met we never got the score rightly settled."

"That was a long time ago, Benko. I'm not here looking for trouble."

The mounting tension and the promise of blood brought the other men off the porch, and Obediah Jones stepped back. An ancient oak tree offered him protection from behind and provided an unexpected coolness in the middle of the busy fort's activities.

"Maybe I am," Tatum said, his voice filled with pent-up aggression. "I don't ferget none too easy."

"This isn't the place, Benko. We...."

Benko Tatum struck, his razor-sharp knife leaving a fine white line along Obediah's jaw that slowly began to moisten with little red beads. The mountain man, soft from a dull winter in St. Louis, had reacted too slowly, and he felt the bite and sting with a mixture of unbelieving surprise and outrage.

Ducking, as Tatum moved in with another savage thrust of his up-turned blade, Obediah brought his fist up almost from the ground hammering it into the underside of Tatum's jaw, snapping the man's head back and slamming him squarely into the dirt. The knife flew from Tatum's hand and landed beneath the frightened and skittish horses tied at the crowded hitching rail.

Stunned from the savage blow, Tatum shook his head

and rolled over, grasping for the blade a few feet beyond his reach. Winded from the unexpected exertion, Obediah lunged toward the prancing, jumping horse in an effort to beat Tatum to the deadly weapon and landed squarely on top of him. The two men rolled in the dirt, each trying to get a solid grip on the other while dodging the flying hooves around them.

Bracing with one foot, Tatum grabbed two fists full of Obediah's hair, rammed his head into the ground, and flipped on top. The man fought like a wild animal, repeatedly pounding Obediah's head in the dirt, giving no advantage as Obediah struggled to get free. Oblivious to anything but his rage, Tatum ignored the flying hooves until one grazed his face, the sharp edge of the iron shoe laying his cheek open. Blood spattered on Obediah's chest and Tatum broke free, grabbing at his torn face. Obediah struggled to his feet and grabbed Tatum's torn shirt, hauling him up for what he hoped would be a finishing blow, but rough hands clamped on his arms and rudely threw Obediah against the broad trunk of the oak tree, holding him fast.

"He ain't goin' nowheres, Benko. Take yer time, this soft-belly's about tuckered out."

Tatum's men held him fast, and Obediah's heart beat so rapidly from anger, exertion, and frustration that Tatum's bloody face swam before him.

Benko Tatum slowly got to his feet, his knife glinting in the low afternoon sun. This was not the first time Obediah Jones had laid hands on him, but it was about to be the last. Holding his bloody cheek, filled with hatred and a seething rage, he staggered toward one of the two men he hated most in this world. "Yer a dead man, Obediah Jones," he croaked, removing his hand and staring unbelievingly at the blood and dirt that covered it. "I'm gonna dump yer boudins in a bloody pile all over yer feet."

The screened door of the Quarter Master's office slammed, and two army officers ran down the steps. "You men there...step back," one shouted. "What's going on here?"

"Let 'im go," Tatum hissed, tucking his knife in his belt.

"Next time," Obediah responded, shaking himself loose and pushing past Tatum toward the building. "We just had a minor disagreement, Lieutenant. Nothing that can't wait."

"Well, it better," one said, as the two officers stepped between Obediah, Tatum, and the others. "But it looks as if that face can't wait. You," he said, pointing to one of Tatum's men, "get that man over to the post surgeon's office. We simply have no time for this."

Motioning to Obediah, the second officer said, "If you're looking for work, there's plenty t' find inside, but we don't need more trouble than we've got."

"No trouble," Tatum growled. "We already got our workin' orders."

"Then why're you standing around here? Get that face fixed. You're needed out there," the Lieutenant said, nodding his head toward the wagons on the parade field. "Get with it."

Obediah mounted the steps to the Quarter Master's building. As he reached for the screened door, he turned to see Benko Tatum staring at him from the edge of the busy parade field. The look on his bloody, distorted face left little doubt that what had started long ago in the mountains to the west was not over.

The large, noisy stock room was cool, despite the

frenetic activity within it, and it had the familiar, comforting smell of canvas, leather, and iron. The large man behind the counter wore a dark blue, sweat-stained tunic with the stripes of a Master Sergeant on its sleeve. His tough but friendly face had a ruddy Irish glow to it that spoke eloquently of a hard life and raucous, good-natured times, and he gave orders to bustling troopers assembling supplies from deep, high-stacked shelves throughout the building with a gusto that seemed a combination of military discipline and motherly concern. He reminded Obediah of a large, red, mother hen: concerned, caring, but not one to trifle with.

"And what exactly might you be wantin'?" the Sergeant said, turning to Obediah and leaning his elbow on the counter. "As if I don't have enough problems this glorious day."

Attempting to wipe the dirt and sweat from his face with the back of his sleeve, Obediah Jones said, "Well...Sergeant...I am headed west...to the mountains, and I...."

"Say no more, lad," the Sergeant said, slapping the counter with his big hand. "I've heard it a million times or more. You want t' be a scout fer the army. Is 'at right, me boy?"

"No, that's not right, Sergeant," Obediah said, leaning across the counter, his face within a few inches of the Sergeant's. "I am a scout, and I am here to offer the United States Army the opportunity of using my services. At a fair price, of course."

"Oh, of course," the Sergeant said, straightening up. "And for that, lad, you'll have t' be talkin' with the officer in charge. Who, I might add, takes no pleasure in talkin' with the likes of you."

"Well, let's you and me leave that up to him. Where exactly might he be found?"

"Well...now...first off, just what exactly makes ya think that it's west we're headin'? We got more'n our share of troubles right here in the Kansas Territory, don't y' know. And, from the looks of your face, it appears you've had some Kansas trouble yer self."

"Now, that's exactly what leads me to believe you are making a big move west. The men I've just had some discussion and a minor disagreement with have little interest in Kansas and its problems."

"Well...it's right ya are," the Sergeant said, taking a deep breath and wiping his hand across his pained face. "These men," he said, jerking his thumb over his shoulder, "and meself...along with a good many more'll be headin' fer Utah t' put down Brigham Young's rebellion. And at great personal sacrifice, I might add."

"Brigham Young's rebel...."

"That's right, lad. And if yer still interested, it's Colonel Alexander ya must see. With all the confusion, nobody knows better than him what's happenin'. And, now lad," he said, turning from Obediah with an air of military dismissal, "I gotta be about m' chores, so be on yer way, now."

"Well...yes, but first, you might tell me where I can find this great man who has all of these answers."

"Oh...'great man', is it? Well, now," the Sergeant said, rubbing his large nose with a stubby finger—an unconscious gesture that signaled a dangerous level of annoyance to those that knew him. "This 'great man' can be found right out that door behind ye."

Obediah turned to follow the Master Sergeant's gaze to

the door he had just entered.

"'Tis a door ya must go through one way or t'other."

The Sergeant's face cracked into a big grin as he turned from Obediah and hollered, "And now, lads, in the heat of the day, let's stop an' have a wee one in gratitude fer our many blessings."

After repeated efforts to speak with Colonel Alexander, it was more than apparent to Obediah Jones that the Colonel had little time for him.

"If you're any good, we can use you," Alexander said, with a wave of dismissal. "Sign up in the usual way, and be ready to move out within a few days. We need a well-scouted route into the Wasatch mountains. One where we can easily defend ourselves."

"Excuse me, Colonel, I know you're busy, but this seems to me to be a crazy notion. I know someth...."

"Now, just a minute Mr....what's your name again?" the Colonel said, looking closely at Obediah for the first time. "Jones, Colonel Alexander. Obediah Jones."

"Yes...well, now look here, Mr. Jones," the officer responded hotly. "What I want is a scout, not a tactician. I'll do that. Do you understand, Mr. Jones?"

"Yes, Colonel, I do, but I know something of the Mormons, and I know the mountains. To begin with, I really can't believe that those people are in any state of rebellion. But, if they are, it's not too likely that you will get into the Salt Lake Valley without their consent."

Colonel Alexander rose behind his desk. "I will spare the time to explain this to you only once, Mr. Jones. I am unconcerned about their consent," he said, emphasizing each word with unfriendly irritation. "And when General Harney gives the order, we will, by thunder, enter that valley one way or the other. And we'll do it with or without Brigham Young's approval. Or yours, for that matter."

"Colonel, there is really only one relatively short way into the Salt Lake Valley, and by the time you get all these troopers and their supplies out in those mountains, there is likely to be little safety from either the Mormons or the weather. Have you thought of that, sir?"

"Now look here, Jones," Alexander said, walking to a wall map. "You are a scout, nothing more. It's your job to help get us from here to here." Emphasizing his words, the officer ran his finger from Ft. Leavenworth to a point on the crude map marked "Great Basin."

"But...sir...."

"No buts, Mr. Jones. The newly elected President of these United States and territories made this decision, wise or not. When, why, or how he did it is no concern of yours...or mine. It is sufficient that he made this decision, and we, by thunder, will carry it out. The man who must answer for its wisdom is James Buchanan."

Chapter Two

The spotlessly white door opened and the newly installed fifteenth President of the United States, James Buchanan, entered his White House office. To the two men that had been patiently waiting for him, along with several of their aides, Buchanan's presence seemed to increase the depressingly sultry atmosphere of the uncomfortably warm room.

It had been a difficult election campaign for the President, and his supporters within the party had been few. Selected as the dark horse candidate after 48 futile ballots in the contentious Democrat convention, and having received only 45 percent of the popular vote in a three-way race that centered on slavery and a rebellious South, Buchanan knew he was not the recipient of any decisive mandate by his bickering party or by his countrymen. He was a man caught in a vice-like grip between slavery, abolition, secession, and expansion. In many ways, he was a man who could not succeed as President and, deep inside, he knew it.

The President crossed the carpeted expanse and sat down at his large, ornate desk. Leaning forward he said, "Mr. Black, what is the purpose of this meeting?"

Jeremiah S. Black, the Attorney General of the United States, rose from his seat, cleared his throat and said, "Mr. President, as you are aware, for months now, complaints have periodically been received from federal officials and others out in the Great Basin, complaining that the Mormons have no respect whatsoever for civil authority.

That, in addition to their many...."

"I'm aware of all of that, Mr. Black," the President interrupted briskly. "So what? Neither do many others out on the frontier, it seems—a wild place, as we all know," he said, leaning back in his chair. "Get on with it, man."

Reaching for a folder on a table near his chair, the Attorney General continued, "Mr. President, to top it off, I have now receiv...."

"Is it hot in this room, gentlemen, or is it just me?" the President broke in, mopping his forehead with an amazingly white, starched handkerchief.

With the exception of the already perspiring and uncomfortable Attorney General, the others mumbled their unanimous acknowledgment of the unusually oppressive atmosphere in the otherwise pleasant room.

The spring of 1857 was proving to be muggy and warm. Many of the city's more affluent residents had already fled for the cooler temperatures of the Virginia hills or the Maryland shore.

"Isaiah!" the President bellowed.

A black liveryman quietly appeared through a door at the rear of the room. "Yessuh?"

"Will you please open some windows and get some air in this room?" the President demanded.

"Yessuh...I'll do ma bes' Mista Pres'dent."

"I tell you, gentlemen, it's a marvel. All I have to do is speak and these people appear like ghosts and do my bidding. I have had servants in private life, but nothing to match some of these White House domestics. You can bet they don't get much in return, either. I can't help but wonder what life would be like if everyone in this city could get things done in such a manner...and for so little," the

President said, his uncomfortable guests glancing at one another, taking further discomfort from the obvious intent of the President's words. "Thank you, Isaiah."

"Yessuh," the black man said, as he left the sultry room and silently closed the enameled door behind him.

"Well...let's get on with it, man."

Jeremiah Black pushed a lengthy, multi-paged letter across the desk toward the Chief Executive.

"What's this?" the President demanded.

"That, sir, is the resignation letter of Judge W. W. Drummond, Justice of the Supreme Court of the Utah Territory. In it he...."

"What's he resigning for?"

"He explains himself in the letter, Mr. President. It would behoove you to read it."

"It would, would it?"

"Indeed, Mr. President. Its allegations constitute the purpose for which we are met here today, sir."

"Hmm," the President responded, as he adjusted his wire reading glasses, and bent over the lengthy document. "He seems to explain himself at some length."

"He does, indeed, sir. But, after reading it, I think you will agree that the circumstances warrant such a...."

"Mm...," the President responded, his attention on the letter before him, his reading punctuated only by frequent grunts and sighs. "Well...this can't...surely not...well, if this...."

"Mr. President, I...."

"Sit down and let me finish, man," the President grumbled irritably.

Annoyed by what he considered the President's lack of respect for his office, if not himself, the Attorney General took his seat to wait patiently with the others.

At length, the President looked up and bellowed, "Isaiah!"

Again, as if from nowhere, the slave appeared. "Mista Pres'dent?"

"Bring us something cold and wet, Isaiah. And plentiful. This meeting may take some time, yet."

"I'll be right back, suh."

The President turned back to the letter on his desk and looked up at the men before him. "Are these allegations true...these things can't be true...can they?"

"We have every reason to believe they are, Mr. President," the Attorney General said.

"Well...just look here," the President sat forward, waving a page of the letter at the Attorney General. "This Drummond fellow is accusing them of systematic murder, of maintaining a secret army or police or whatever. Why, I can't...I just...."

"Mr. President, Judge Drummond has been out there in the Utah Territory for some time. He surely would have no reason to make such accusations with no provocation, and we all know the history of these bothersome and disagreeable...."

"Well, if they...."

"Mr. President, may I say something, sir?" The hitherto silent Secretary of War, John B. Floyd, rose from his chair.

"Well?"

"Of course these accusations are true. As the Attorney General says, we all know what the history of these Mormons has been. They've been trouble since that Smith fellow had his first visions. Everywhere they've gone, his hallucinations have caused trouble...New York,

Illinois...Missouri was a bloody mess, thanks to them. And, now they're out in Utah keeping women in slavery and following the every word of that tyrant Brigham Young. Why...he's supposed to be some sort of prophet. They dote on...."

"We needn't rehearse all of that," the Attorney General broke in. "We...."

"Well, what's the point, gentlemen? How can I be concerned with charges of slavery or whatever out there when it threatens to tear us all apart right here? And even if there is truth to these allegations, what is expected of me?" the President snapped. "What am I supposed t'...."

"Mr. President," the Secretary of War responded, "I say we send troops out there and put an end once and for all to this religious foolishness."

"You mean, send an army out there, Mr. Floyd?"

"I do, sir."

"And do what? Kill every man, woman, and child?"

"Well...I...."

"And on what pretense? Do we do it on the basis of these kinds of allegations? Are they invading us? Is this secret band of criminals...these...what did he call them?" the President asked, grabbing a page of the letter from his desk.

"Danites, sir."

"Yes...Danites. Are they, or some Mormon army of assassins, invading us?" the President asked, incredulously.

"No sir...but...the slander of federal officials...."

"We can't do something like that just because we get reports of their not speaking well of us, Mr. Floyd."

"No, sir, but murders and...."

"Mr. President, if I may, sir," the Attorney General said, rising from his chair, "these allegations are serious. And there is no question that something must be done."

"I've gotten that far, Mr. Attorney General. The question is, what?" the President said peevishly. "Within reason, that is."

The room became quiet as the slave unexpectedly entered, the unnatural silence broken only by the merry tinkling of large glasses of iced tea, a fragrant sprig of mint protruding from each. The slave crossed the room and placed the tray on the President's desk.

"That's fine, Isaiah," the President mumbled. "Now, leave us."

"Yessuh," the black man responded, as he quietly left the room.

"Mr. President, these are not the only allegations. We hear almost daily complaints. McGraw's letter last year indicated that things...."

"Yes, yes, I know all of that."

"Mr. President, we...."

"Look, gentlemen, the realities are that I have Kansas to worry about, with troops out there. How would I look sending an army from Kansas to invade the Mormons while arguing for popular sovereignty? Answer me that!"

"But...Mr. President, we...."

"But nothing! We talk of letting Kansas and the other territories determine for themselves whether they want slavery or not, we talk of local choice, and you are telling me that we should invade the Utah Territory. The sense of that eludes me, gentlemen."

"Mr. President," the Attorney General responded hotly, "something must be done. Brigham Young's notion of popular sovereignty seems to include the evils of slavery and polygamy."

"Well...in part, so does ours, Mr. Black."

"But, sir, Young can't be left to his own devices to the embarrassment of this administration, sir."

"Mr. Black," the President said, as if speaking to a rebellious child, "Kansas is likely to be this administration's greatest embarrassment, if not the nation's. If I fail to bring Kansas into the union as a free state and persuade the South that I am not antislavery and to acquiesce, then we will have embarrassment, Mr. Black. We'll have war, that's what we'll have. And you want me to send troops to the other side of the continent?"

"Mr. President," the Secretary of War broke in, "if we could just...."

"Let me finish, Mr. Floyd." the President interrupted. "We are at as dangerous a trespass as this nation has ever been. Just when I feel rebellion has been obviated, other sectionist problems seem to erupt. Why, just look at this Dred Scott thing. Who knows what that's going to bring? Taney was right, but now secession is spoken of openly in the Senate—on a daily basis. The South's threats seem never to cease. Now, on top of all of this, you bring me the Mormons.

"What am I to do, gentlemen? I have precious little power in this office, as you know. What am I to do with the Southern states? They simply must acquiesce. I have no way of stopping them, let alone these Mormons on the other side of the continent," the President said, waving his hand in dismissal of the idea.

"The Constitution's silent on these kinds of matters, gentlemen. I'm relatively helpless. What's to prevent that

Brigham Young fellow from just declaring his state of Deseret an independent nation? Tell me that!"

The Attorney General slumped down in his chair. "Well, perhaps we could at least relieve Young as Territorial Governor and replace him and his appointed officials with our own people."

The President stared at his Attorney General for a long moment. "Now, that," he said, slowly, "is perhaps a more sensible solution. One we could even pursue with some vigor."

"But, Mr. President," Floyd responded, "what have we to believe that your new appointees will be accepted by the Mormons? What's to prevent them from being murdered, too?"

"That's true, too," the President said, sinking back in his chair, drumming his desk with his fingers. "Apparently they are a war-like bunch of heathens."

"We still must send troops," the Secretary of War said.

"But, hang it man, Congress is out of session, and I've got all...."

"Perhaps, with Congress out of town, now is precisely the time to act," the Attorney General responded. "Given the extremely serious nature of these problems, you won't have the political flack to worry about. We can get things going and have a small expeditionary force out there this summer, install our people, and have it done before the snow flies."

"No one can fault you for that," said the Secretary of War. "That highbinder, Brigham Young, will be in his place, peace will have been restored, and you'll be seen as the man who got it done."

"You'll have no trouble from Congress," the Attorney

General said, with undue enthusiasm. "Not once this is done."

"By Jove, you may be right," the President said, leaning forward. "You know, when you stop to think about it...it could give the appearance of decisiveness at the very time such messages need to be sent."

The President slumped back in his chair lost in thought, and then said, "But if we fail, if we fail...."

"We will not fail, Mr. President," Secretary Floyd responded. "This will be handled swiftly and decisively."

"Very well, gentlemen." The President rose from his desk. "I want this expeditiously accomplished—with as small a force as possible—and I want to know what's happening at every step. Is that clear?"

" Yes sir, it is," Black responded.

"Is that absolutely clear, Mr. Floyd?"

"Indeed it is, sir."

"Then, done it is," the President said, waving his hand in apparent dismissal. "Thank you, gentlemen."

As the men left the room, the newly installed President, not yet accustomed to what little power he thought he had, and overwhelmed with the gravity of his problems, leaned back in his chair and stretched his cramped legs. The room had not been this quiet all morning. He hoped the same could be said for his fractious nation by the end of summer.

"It had better be, gentlemen. It had better be," he said to himself.

CHAPTER THREE

Old habits die hard and Jasper Pughsey sat well back in the tree line, a lone figure surveying the celebration the Saints, as they called themselves, were enjoying.

The mountain man, disdainful of the unwanted invasion of the west by humanity and its flotsam, could not help but admire this breed of determined pioneers. They deserved their day of jubilee—even in his cherished wilderness.

It was the 24th of July, 1857, a day of true celebration and gratitude for ten hard years on the frontier, free from the molestations of the past. Looking back, it seemed a short, though difficult, time since they had entered their beloved valley of the Great Salt Lake and established a modern civilization where none but the most primitive had ever existed before. Out of the bleak Western desert, where so short a time ago only jack rabbits and snakes had eked out a meager living, a city had arisen, and the most remote areas of the Western North American continent were being subdued into the State of Deseret. The sun-splashed peaks surrounding the high mountain valley rang with the noise of brass bands and the loud, exuberant voices of the celebrants. On two of those rocky crags, the stars and stripes had been unfurled, as they had from the tops of several tall pine trees within the encampment.

"Jest look," the old mountain man muttered to himself, "ain't no peace t' be found nowhere." From his shady, solitary vantage point, he could survey the entire encampment surrounding Silver Lake. Three large boweries, each complete with wooden floors, were encompassed by tents and a sea of happy humanity. Everywhere he looked something seemed to be happening: bands were playing, speeches were being given, and large amounts of food were being consumed from countless tables that labored under their mouth-watering burdens.

Jasper's stomach grumbled with jealousy. "Well, ma'be it ain't all bad," he grunted, as he rose, stretched his cramped legs, and mounted his horse. "Cum'on," he said, nudging the reluctant animal, "let's go be sociable-like...fer a time, anyways."

As the mountain man descended from his place of concealment through a small stand of aspen and into the meadow that lay between him and the busy encampment, a light wagon pulled by a double span of lathered horses clattered over a rise and came to a dusty stop in front of him.

Jasper's horse shied and reared from the dust and rocks thrown by the big team as the animals clamored to a grateful stop, their sides heaving from their frantic race up Big Cottonwood Canyon. "What in tarnation?" he hollered, as he fought to calm his startled mount.

"Where's President Young?" yelled a big man, as he jumped from the wagon where two companions remained. "I said...where's President Young?"

Jasper Pughsey looked into two of the most piercing, pale, blue eyes he had ever seen. The man was solidly set and seemed big, though he was of no more than average height. He had a high, broad forehead, and black hair spilled onto his back, obscuring his cotton shirt; his broad, demanding face was nearly hidden by a beard that seemed never to have known a blade. It didn't take much experience to know this was a thoroughly dangerous man, one whose will would not be easily thwarted. The mountain man liked him immediately.

"I said...."

"I heard," Jasper replied irritably. "He's over there," he said, his hand sweeping the crowded, lively basin before them.

Orrin Porter Rockwell grabbed the reins of Jasper's horse and seemed to pull the animal up to him. "Mister, we've come a long way in a big hurry and I ain't in no mood...."

Rockwell's two companions jumped from the wagon as an angry Jasper Pughsey began to dismount. "Now's not the time, Orrin," hollered one.

Porter Rockwell dropped the reins and turned back to the wagon, "Then you tell 'im, Brother Smoot," he said, "we've got little time."

"We've got t' find the Prophet fast...there may be little time. We...."

"Well, then...what in tarnation is it?" Jasper said, resettling himself in his saddle.

"It looks like war. There's an army headed our way and its apparent intention is to wipe us out—man, woman, and child."

Jasper reined his horse around. "Well, why didn't ya say so? I'll he'p ya find 'im."

The gentle, cool breeze that moved through the open ends of the wooden-floored tent did little to stifle the oppressive atmosphere that surrounded its occupants. The man who would become known as the great American colonizer, the Prophet of the Latter-day Saints, sat slumped in a hard, wooden chair behind a makeshift desk listening to the report of the four men standing before him, his anger mounting. Hearing all he could stand, Brigham Young slammed his big fist on the desk, startling the messengers to silence.

"Enough!"

The Prophet rose, bowing his head beneath the low tent roof and strode to the open tent flap where he moodily watched the unsuspecting Saints as they enjoyed their day of rest and celebration. Filling his lungs with the clean mountain air, he turned and said, "When will this people be left in peace? How much must they endure? What must they do to prove their value and loyalty to the American nation?"

Warming to his thoughts, the big man swept the tiny room with his hand, "What have we harmed? Look at what we have accomplished. The West has become accessible to the United States, largely because of the courage and imagination of Saints such as these. Our men have served without complaint in the nation's army, leaving their families to suffer untold hardships. There are settlements from here to San Diego. What on earth do they want of us? To renounce our faith? Our God? To change our religion to suit their prejudices?"

The Prophet returned to his desk, sat down, and leaned forward. "Well, by the Eternal, it will not happen," he said, jabbing the desk viciously with his finger. "Come what may, here we make our stand! We tolerate no more!"

Jasper Pughsey, standing at the rear of the tent, had seen that look on men's faces before, but not quite like this: it was the look of living rock, of solid, unyielding determination. There were moments in the affairs of men when black clouds hung low, the wind blew cold, and the weather turned fit for neither man nor beast. At such perilous times, smart was the man or animal who sought the most secure shelter. Lightning split the oldest, tallest, and strongest of pines; grizzlies tore one another to pieces for no reason; the faces of redmen were covered with the paint of war. Such an atmosphere was this, and Jasper Pughsey knew that it forbode only the worst of times.

"Joseph was right, you know," Brigham Young continued. "They can no more stop us than stay the mighty Missouri with their puny hands." The Prophet leaned back and seemed to relax, his chair creaking with his weight. "Still they try...no sense in them, it would seem."

Looking into the face of this man, Jasper Pughsey knew it was true. Furthermore, for some reason he could not fathom, or did not want to fathom, he was glad to be where he was right at this moment. Jasper studied the strong face of this leader...this President...this...whatever else they chose to call him. He held back the thought, but it came despite his effort—this Prophet.

Regardless of the anger displayed in the stubborn, rugged face, there was a kind of glow to the man's features, an air of invincibility about the Mormon leader. Instinctively, the mountain man knew that this was a man to reckon with, a man to follow. Beneath all that strength lay a wisdom that made him an anvil. Pound as his enemies would, use whatever force they could muster—blade, ball, and cannon—Jasper Pughsey knew that Brigham Young and his people would stand. This man was surely the right hand of the Almighty.

CHAPTER FOUR

With the on-set of evening, an unseasonably cold wind began blowing up the canyon and through the tall pines, stirring the willows along the banks of Silver Lake, and breaking up the brilliant reflection of the rocky peaks, red in the glow of the setting sun.

The Saints, weary from the day's festivities and subdued by the rumors of an invading army, began assembling at the largest of the arbors. Few, if any, had doubts of what was to come. Brother Brigham would know what to do; he had warned them. The dreadful news of the advancing army was not entirely unexpected, and nearly everyone knew that none of the Federal appointees that had squatted in Deseret during the past ten years was to be trusted.

If there was to be war, so be it. There was nowhere else to go, and not a man or woman among them was of a mind to give up the hard-fought progress of the past ten years. The tops of the mountains had provided the struggling Saints with safety from the world up to this very day, and under the leadership of this Prophet, whatever the sacrifice, here they would make their stand. The Prophet had said as much before, and there was no reason to think that anything had changed.

Jasper Pughsey leaned against the fragrant, sharp-edged bark of a large pine tree, not too far from the gathering assembly. Chewing contemplatively on a long pine needle and enjoying its strong, gummy taste, he watched the large crowd begin singing praise to their Prophet—which one he was not quite sure.

"Danged if I ain't never seen the likes of it," Jasper grunted, as he turned to leave. "No time fer this child t' stay around these parts."

"Thinkin' of leavin' just when things promise t' get interesting real quick-like?"

The big, bearded man stepped from the gathering darkness among the pines into Jasper Pughsey's path, surprising the usually cautious mountain man with his sudden appearance. Nothing irritated Jasper more than being caught off guard.

"Well, now, I figger I got my reasons, an' yew got yours, an' they ain't necessarily similar," Jasper shot back, a little too hotly.

Porter Rockwell stepped around the mountain man and motioned toward the assembled Saints. "Look't them folks. If you ever seen a more determined bunch, I wanna know where. They're into it up t' here," he said, drawing his thumb across his throat.

"Seems so," Jasper replied, anxious to be on his way. "Ain't got nothin' t' do with me, anyways."

"I know better'n that. I can tell by lookin' at ya, you've blacked your face a time 'r two when things got grievous. Besides, I saw yer look back in President Young's tent."

Jasper, ever open to the suggestion of approval, relaxed and followed Rockwell's gaze. "Well...ma'be so...but this ain't my dust-up."

"They ain't gonna lose in this scrap, ya know."

"Yeah...well, ma'be," Jasper allowed.

"They can't, man. Stop an' think. I hear tell you been around these parts a while."

"They've come a spell," Jasper, agreed. "I done some with 'em."

"I've heard tell," Rockwell said, giving Jasper a sideways glance. "That's the reason you know as well as I know, they ain't gonna lose. Such as that just ain't in 'em."

"Some truth t' that," Jasper agreed.

"They come outta the jaws of hell t' settle in these mountains. They got nowhere t' go. Stayin' here's the only option we got—army 'r no."

In the arbor, the crowd grew quiet as Brigham Young rose and stepped to the make-shift pulpit a few yards from the two grim disputants, their forms lost in the darkening tree line. As the Prophet of the Latter-day Saints paused to gather his thoughts, nothing could be heard but the wind giving the forest the deep sound of the wild, pine-clad mountains both men had come to love as home.

"Besides," Rockwell said, "we got something that army ain't got."

"What's thet?"

"Him," he said, nodding his head in the direction of the Mormon Prophet.

"Before we leave this peaceful setting, I have a few things I need to say. I don't want to say them, but they need to be said," the Prophet began. "Not too many years ago, a young man joined the Church, and he said that he came into the Church mad and has been mad ever since."

Brigham Young paused, and the crowd strained not to miss his next words. "Well, I'm angry, too. Almost too angry to be standing here trying to talk to you.

"I don't need to rehearse things to you. Twenty-five years and more we've been driven from place to place. Driven, scattered, and peeled—and every time without provocation," Brigham Young said, his voice rising. "Our only crime was being united, obeying the laws of the land,

and striving to worship our God. And now they are organizing their forces to come here and protect infernal scamps who are anxious to come and kill whom they please, destroy whom they please, and finally exterminate the 'Mormons.'"

The Prophet paused, as the assembled Saints murmured their agreement.

"We have transgressed no law," he continued, suddenly slamming his fist onto the pulpit. "We have had no occasion to do so, neither do we intend to, but as for any nation coming to destroy this people, God Almighty being my helper, they cannot come!"

The walls of the canyon echoed with loud approval as the Saints reacted to their leader's anger, frustration, and determination. This was the man that had led them west; this was the man that had inspired the sacrifices that built an empire in ten short, painful years, and this man would see them to victory against whatever force the adversary could send against them.

"Ten years ago, this very day," the Prophet continued, "whilst speaking to the brethren, I said, inadvertently, if the people of the United States will let us alone for ten years, we will ask no odds of them. And ten years from that very day, we have a message brought by Brothers Smoot, Stoddard, and Rockwell, that the Government has stopped the mail, and that they have ordered 2,500 troops to come here and hold the Mormons still, while priests, politicians, speculators and whoremongers, and every mean, filthy character that could be raked up should come here and kill us off."

Brigham Young paused for what seemed an eternity. The crowd appeared to lean as one toward their leader, anxious not to miss his next words. The words came with cold authority—each laid down as a law in itself.

"Well, mind you this: In the name of Israel's God, we ask no odds of them!"

The bowery erupted with the din of loud approval.

Jasper Pughsey spat into the weeds at his feet. "Damned if I ever heard the likes of thet," he said, scratching the grizzled stubble that covered his chin. "What's gonna happen now?"

"Just listen," Rockwell whispered.

"We have borne enough of their hellish abuse, and we will not bear any more of it," Brigham Young continued, as the excited Saints sank into their seats. His voice grew soft and everyone present strained to catch his words. "No law requires any further forbearance on our part.

"Return in the morning to your homes in the Valley of the Great Salt Lake. Under my direction, the Nauvoo Legion will prepare to meet the enemy and do that which is necessary to see that the invaders are stopped."

The Saints stood as the Prophet left the stand, followed by his counselors and other Church leaders.

"See what I mean?" the bearded man said. "Ain't no time t' be leavin'."

"He's some awright," Jasper said. "Time was we'd have said he had the ha'r of the b'ar in 'im. Wagh!"

"Yep," responded Rockwell. "That's a man t' reckon with, and he's a man t' fight with. Whadda you think?" Cold eyes stared hard at Jasper Pughsey. "What I've heard of you, you're one t' recognize what's needful."

The old mountain man knew a good time when he saw one coming, though he liked to pick his quarrels carefully. "Well, I ain't one t' watch whilst good people get kicked around, alright," Jasper said. "But it appears t' me that army's gonna have plenty t' deal with where these folks's concerned."

"You got that straight, but we need help from them that's got savvy. You know these mountains as well, if not better, than any man jack amongst us, and I'd take it right personal if ya'd not run off just yet."

"Well...."

"Cum'on, then," Porter Rockwell said, nudging Jasper's arm. "Come with me."

Late one morning, a week after the Saints had trudged down the canyon from their aborted celebration, Porter Rockwell and Jasper Pughsey dismounted in a large stand of cottonwood and Box Elder trees near the mouth of Emigration Canyon.

The week had been one filled with rumors and stories of the threatened invasion. Church leaders were in meetings daily, planning for what appeared to be the inevitable. And, though Jasper Pughsey had been included in very few of them, Porter Rockwell kept him abreast of developments.

Finally, the two had spent most of the morning packing an extra horse for a trip that the secretive Rockwell said might last several weeks.

"This here is Emigration Canyon," Rockwell said, leading his horse to the noisy, tumbling stream nearby. "It's where we first entered the valley—other canyons're too steep and filled with brush and trees. We'll meet Lot Smith here."

Jasper's horse dipped its muzzle into the cold, rushing water. "I know these mountains and I know where I am, but what I don't know," the irritated mountain man responded, "is jest who this Lot Smith feller is, anyways?"

"You're gonna like Lot, Pughsey," Rockwell responded, ignoring Jasper's ill temper. "He's just like me an' you— knows the lay of things."

"Yew leave it t' me t' decide who I like an' who I don't," Jasper Pughsey said, settling himself on a large rock. "What I don't like is bein' kept in the dark about what's goin' on. Once I'm in, I expect t' stay in."

"Best fer Lot Smith t' tell ya. He spent most of the week, night'n day, with Brother Brigham and the brethren figgerin' things out. They've got a plan, and you and me are gonna.... Here he comes now," Rockwell said, getting to his feet.

An increasingly skeptical Jasper Pughsey watched the much younger man ride into the clearing and dismount. Walking rapidly toward Jasper and Rockwell, Lot Smith thrust his hand in Jasper's direction and said, "Hello...I'm Major Lot Smith."

The mountain man accepted the friendly gesture, but dropped Smith's hand quickly.

Attempting to stifle a chuckle, Jasper responded, "Major?" He looked toward Porter Rockwell with a twinkle in his eye, "Well, now...jest what're yew a Major of, exactly?"

"Well...exactly," Smith responded amiably, "I'm a Major of the Nauvoo Legion, for whom I hope you are going to do some scouting. And, the fact is, if what Orrin, here, tells me is true, we need you."

"Well...I don't know what ya told 'im," Jasper said, looking at Rockwell with a quick wink, "but sounds like it must have been true enough. I sure...."

"Well, now," Rockwell interjected, "don't you go get...."

"What we need now gentlemen is information, and we need it badly," Smith said, returning to his horse and withdrawing a thin leather pouch from his saddle bag.

Jasper Pughsey and Porter Rockwell followed the Mormon officer to a large, flat rock away from the noise of the stream, where he unfolded a crudely drawn map and spread it out as flatly as possible.

"We've got to know where that army is and what its intentions are before we can be certain how to respond," the Major said, looking up at his two scouts. "We know they are coming, and we know there is only one way they can come. But we're guessing as to just how large they are, what kind of equipment they are bringing with them, and how quickly they can get here."

"It'll take 'em weeks, if not months," Jasper said, with a grunt. "An' seems t' me they're startin' out a might late in the season fer such a trek."

"Seems so to us, too, Mr. Pughsey," Smith responded. "But, near as we can tell, the first contingents left Fort Leavenworth nearly three weeks ago. That means," the Major said, thumping the map with his forefinger, "that army could be through South Pass...maybe as early as the middle of September."

Jasper drew a deep breath, let it out slowly, and said, "Thet time of year in thet high country could prove t' be a might spiteful. If the weather's right, yew...."

"We mean t' make it more'n spiteful, weather or no," Rockwell broke in. "From here t' here," he said, running a stubby finger along the map from the Green River on its right-hand margin to a spot in the middle marked Echo Canyon, "they're goin' to know they got more'n the weather t' worry over. And right here," he emphasized, stabbing at the map, "is where they ain't goin' no furtherr. Not without Brother Brigham's approval."

"Port's right, Mr. Pughsey. We've got nowhere to go, therefore we are going nowhere. And right there," the Major said, pointing to Echo canyon, "is the choke point."

"So, what's needful fer you an' me is to find out as much as we can, and get that information right back here. Then the fun's gonna begin. You with us?" Rockwell asked, an edge to his voice.

"I said I was, didn't I," Jasper responded irritably.

"Good," the Major said. "Then take this map and bring as much information back to us as you can, as quickly as you can."

CHAPTER FIVE

A line of violent thunder showers had passed during the night, and the early morning sun made the dense, wet prairie grass glitter in the light breeze. The grass rustled with a free and soothing sound as the soft, fresh wind moved it in waves around the shanks of the browsing horses, and they tore and chomped with contentment as they filled their empty stomachs.

In a wide, grassy swale not far away, Jasper Pughsey and Orrin Porter Rockwell carefully surveyed a large, empty camp site, walking from the cold ashes where one fire had been and on to the next, studying the tracks that matted the grass and packed the damp earth.

"Mules...wagons...lots of 'em awright," Rockwell mumbled to himself.

"Uh-huh. Looks like supplies mostly, with troopers protecting the stuff," Jasper responded.

"My guess is they're headin' fer Ham's Fork. That'll probably be where they bunch up fer their push on into Great Salt Lake," Rockwell said, settling himself on a large rock near a blackened fire pit. "In a hurry, too. From what we've seen the past day 'r two, looks like they're pushin' pretty hard...makin' good time."

Jasper Pughsey continued examining the layout of the large camp site, studying tracks, the placement of cook fires and tents. Occasionally he would stop and scowl at some arcane omen left in the earth.

"What's eatin' at ya?" Rockwell asked. "Yer as nervous as a coyote stealin' chickens."

"I'm startin' t' feel more like one of the chickens," Jasper answered as he walked past his puzzled companion and climbed the low hill that flanked the encampment.

"Well...what in tarnation is it?" Rockwell demanded, as he joined Jasper at the top of the hill.

The mountain man crossed his legs, lowered himself to the earth, and pondered the situation. Finally he said, "Well, jest look at how things's laid out." Waving his hand across the camp site he continued, "Every camp we've looked at had the same kinda sign to it."

"So, what," Rockwell retorted. "It's just another army encampment, ain't it."

"Ma'be...ma'be not," Jasper answered, thoughtfully.

"An what's that supposed t' mean?" his dark, bearded companion demanded. "Pughsey...there's times you can be plain intolerable."

"These folks's in a hurry awright," Jasper said, scratchin' his grizzled chin, "but this ain't just a bunch a troopers in a hurry. Somebody's givin' 'em a edge. Somebody knows how t' make the lay a things work fer 'em and not allowin' fer too much carelessness. And fer a bunch this big, and in this big a hurry, that oughta be kinda troublesome t' ya."

Rockwell settled himself in the grass next to Jasper and brushing the long hair away from his face said, "Well...now ya talk of it...it...."

"But what's troublin' me most is there's a lot down there that looks familiar t' me, but I ain't just sure what it is."

"Like fer instance?" the dark man asked.

"Like fer instance, they always camp in a low depression like this one, with plenty a grass fer their animals. They ain't out where their fires can be seen fer any distance, and along the way they gather dry fuel so's their fires make little smoke. A half a mile away, er even less, an' you'd never know they was here."

"We found 'em."

"Only 'cause we knew about where they'd be, and we were lookin'."

Orrin Porter Rockwell's hand became lost in his long beard as he scratched his chin contemplatively. "Why d' ya suppose a force this size would bother like that? They're plenty big enough t' discourage any Indians that might be about, if there was any. Why're they bein' s' all fired careful out here?"

"Thet's what's troublin' me," Jasper said, squinting off to the west. "They got some savvy scouts thet know what they're doin'. They go straight from one camp t' the next—no wanderin' around lookin'. Each camp's like the last, hidden as possible and defensible. This ain't no bunch a pork eaters, I'll say thet fer 'em."

"This here army's beginnin' t' look more'n more dangerous, ain't it?"

Benko Tatum leaned across his saddle horn squinting into the distance, annoyed by the glare of the sun in his eyes. Dismounting, he knelt beside a large rock and steadied himself as he brought a small, battered telescope to his eye.

"Well, well, well...if that don't look like my ol' pal Jasper Pughsey—damnation, he's supposed t've gone under," he hissed through his yellow teeth. "Hanged if'n I know who that other pork eater is with 'im, though," he mumbled.

A few hundred yards below him, and well out on the

prairie, Jasper Pughsey and Orrin Porter Rockwell cantered along carefully studying the fresh tracks made by Alexander's advanced units.

Tatum remounted and leaned back in his saddle, his hand automatically stealing to the stock of the treasured Hawken long rifle jutting from the scabbard secured beneath his right leg. "Ugh," he grunted, "a bit too fer. When this child makes 'is move, it'll be real final-like...and I know jest the place."

Wheeling his horse to the right, for a brief time Tatum trotted along the ridge parallel to the two riders below, staying back among the trees and scrub brush. Familiar with the trail and knowing the location of the army, he angled deeper into the trees and spurred his horse to a gallop in an effort to find a secure vantage point ahead of the two scouts.

"Somebody up there's tryin' t' be downright sneaky," Rockwell observed casually.

"Appears so," Jasper responded, as he reined in his horse and dismounted. "Needs t' be more careful with shiny things on sech a sunny day."

Rockwell joined Jasper and the two appeared to be studying something on the ground. Over Rockwell's shoulder, Jasper had a clear view of the ridge line, and he studied it carefully.

"Whaddaya figger?" Rockwell asked.

"Sun spark off a telescope, prob'ly...can't rightly tell...too far."

The two stood, and remounting, each studied the ridge line quickly but carefully, scanning the distant trees and brush for any sign of movement.

"Army scout?" Rockwell asked.

"'ppears so...but why scout back?"

"Injuns?"

"Ain't been no sign t' speak of."

"My guess is he's moved on," Rockwell said, studying the tracks ahead.

"'ppears so," Jasper said. "Best we keep our heads up. I got this itchy feelin' 'is intentions might not be altogether honorable. We might jest meet 'im...."

"Well then...maybe we oughta do a little switchin' 'bout now, huh?"

Jasper looked at his bearded companion in mock surprise. "Times when your gumption gets plain spacious."

"Kinda like a hungry coyote, huh?"

"Similar."

"Well," Rockwell said, as the two spurred their mounts in a gallop toward the brush covered bluff, "let's you an' me sniff that chicken out and pull 'is feathers."

Obediah Jones rode up to Colonel Edmund Brooke Alexander at the head of a long, dusty column of troops and wagons. Bringing his horse to a trot alongside the Colonel's, he said, "There's an excellent camp site about a mile or so ahead. Plenty of water and grass and protected by surrounding bluffs."

"It's early...we could still make a few more miles, Jones," the Colonel said, his voice loud in competition with the noise of the column behind them.

"Yes sir, but the country's getting higher, and tomorrow's march will be tougher and farther to water. What you lose today, you're going to be forced to make tomorrow."

"How far to Fort Laramie?"

"From here...I'd say...two more days. Maybe three. We're making pretty good time, though. From there, or at least from Devil's Gate, we should consider ourselves to be in Mormon country."

Colonel Alexander twisted in his saddle to face his scout directly. "Mormon country?" he said, in reproof. "Let me remind you, Mr. Jones, this is United States territory, not Mormon country."

"Begging your pardon, Colonel, but you'll have to explain that to them, not me."

"That we will do, Mr. Jones. That we will do," Alexander repeated with emphasis.

"Well...my guess is they know right where we sit right this moment...our numbers...and...."

"That's nonsense, sir. I don't...."

The hollow echoes of a rifle shot pulsated over the nearby bluffs bringing the argument to an abrupt conclusion as Colonel Alexander threw his arm in the air ordering the column to a halt.

"Probably Tatum shooting a deer or something," Obediah offered. "I'll...."

"Your friend Tatum is not the least gun shy, Jones," the Colonel said, sarcastically.

"No friend of mine, as you well know Colonel. I'll check it out," Obediah said, slapping his horse's rump with his hat. "With any luck he shot himself in the foot."

"Sergeant O'Riley," the Colonel hollered over his shoulder, "two troopers with Mr. Jones! Smartly, please!" Turning in his saddle, he muttered to himself, "Should never have brought that worthless Tatum along. I don't want anything happening to Jones, the best scout I've ever had. Especially one who knows the enemy as he seems to."

"You did that on purpose," Rockwell said with disgust.

"Corse I did," Jasper shot back, rising from behind a large outcropping of rock where he and Porter Rockwell had watched their potential assailant take up his obvious ambush position. Finding the man's tracks at the top of the bluff, the two had carefully followed them until, glimpsing the man through the trees and scrub brush as he dismounted to make his furtive preparations, they had beaten him at his own craven game.

"Ya only winged 'im...knocked 'im cold. Ya shoulda killed 'em," Rockwell said grudgingly.

"Well, now...as I recall, it was yew and Lot Smith said no one was t' get hurt," Jasper said, his irritation growing. "Oughtn't ya t' make up yer mind?"

"Well," Rockwell responded with equal irritation, "sometimes I've been known t' get fergetful."

"I've heard."

"Besides...he was layin' fer us. If we'd rode around that bluff, he was fixed to blow the two of us out of our saddles."

"True. Let's go down and see who that feller might be. Sort of match 'im up t' 'is intentions," Jasper said, as the two returned to their horses, hidden in the brush not far away.

Approaching cautiously, Porter Rockwell stayed mounted and laid his rifle across his legs, covering the man crumpled face down in the brown bunch grass.

Jasper dismounted and nudged the man over on his back with the toe of his boot, like a man rolling over a log that might have a rattlesnake coiled beneath it. "This feller looks...well I'll be hog swallered if..."

"What's the matter...who...?"

"...if this coon ain't Benko Tatum," Jasper said with an unbelieving snicker.

Porter Rockwell dismounted and joined Jasper peering down at the unconscious man at their feet. "Kinda ugly, ain't 'e. Figger he's dead? He's bled some."

"He ain't dead...not Tatum. Yew ever tried t' kill a snake that just kept crawlin' under rocks?" Jasper said, squatting down beside Tatum. "He might not come around fer a while, and when he does, he's goin' t' know he's got a hurtin' head between them ears...but this snake ain't dead."

"Question is," Rockwell said, pushing the hair from his face, "why was 'e layin' fer us? You figger he's with that outfit up ahead?"

Jasper stood up, stretching his cramped legs. "I suppose. But if he recognized me, it was reason enough fer him. He's threatened to put me under fer a long time now...me an' Obediah Jones. He jest ain't had the right opportunity yet."

"Looks like 'e missed it again...at least where you're concerned," Rockwell said, mounting his horse. "You could put an end to it right now, Pughsey."

Jasper looked up at the dark, bearded man. "What's thet supposed t' mean, Rockwell?"

"Should I fetch a stick and draw ya a picture in the dirt?" Rockwell spat.

"Ain't my way t' kill a man like thet," Jasper shot back. "Even a snake like Benko Tatum, deservin' as he may be, oughta get better'n thet."

"Whaddaya mean, it ain't your way? That feller was about t' kill the both of us, an' he's scoutin' fer that bunch of army scum up ahead. I ought t' do it m'self...right here an' now," Rockwell said, his hand resting on the butt of his holstered Navy Colt.

Jasper Pughsey stepped between the increasingly hostile Rockwell and Benko Tatum, sprawled in the dirt at his feet. "I said, it ain't my way, Rockwell."

Porter Rockwell allowed his body to relax, his hand moving to the saddle horn, and said, "Times when I ain't sure your heart's in this, Pughsey. Times when...."

"Ain't my heart needs t' concern you, Port Rockwell. My head's where its suppose t' be. Thet's what...."

Rockwell suddenly stood in his stirrups, and said, "'ppears we got us some visitors."

"Best we scat," Jasper said, quickly mounting his horse at the unwelcome sound of rapidly approaching horses. "Ain't no point in our gettin' too acquainted jest yet."

"Over here, Jones," the trooper yelled. "Looks like somebody done Tatum in."

Obediah Jones dismounted and walked through the thick brush to where the two troopers stood looking at Tatum's inert body.

"Don't get too near 'im. You're walking all over the sign," he said, tying his horse to some branches a few paces away. Studying the ground, he slowly walked up to Tatum.

"Somebody done it to 'im good," one of the troopers casually observed.

"Yeah...almost too good," Obediah agreed.

A neat, bloody furrow creased Tatum's scalp from above his right ear across his hairless skull.

"Not too deep, and not too shallow," Obediah murmured

to himself, as he knelt by Tatum's body.

"Is 'e dead?"

"Whoever did this didn't want to kill 'im."

"How can y' tell?"

"Because whoever did the job was too close t' miss with a rifle that'd make a furrow that wide," he said, getting up and walking off into the brush. "Nine'll get ya ten it was a Hawken or a Sharps in the hands of an artist. Stay there."

Obediah Jones climbed a small ridge and disappeared into the undergrowth and pinion, emerging at the top of a nearby bluff fifty yards off. "And right here behind these rocks is where they were," he hollered.

"They?" the two troopers asked in unison.

"Yep...two of them," Obediah hollered, as he slid down the steep embankment. "And if whoever fired that shot wanted Benko Tatum dead, you wouldn't see where he was shot, because what was left of his head would be splattered all over this hillside," he said rejoining the two soldiers. "Nobody misses with a Hawken at this range. Nobody that carries a Hawken, at least."

"He's alive, alright," one of the troopers said, squatting beside the bald scout.

"Uh-huh," Obediah responded, mounting his horse. "Let's report back to the Colonel."

"But what about Tatum, here?"

"He'll find his way back. Might take an hour or two, but he'll survive. Always has, at least."

"But it seems kinda...."

"Don't worry about it soldier." Obediah spurred his horse. "I've seen that old snake slither out of worse spots than he's in right now."

Obediah Jones and the two troopers rode into the

confusion of an army setting up camp. The command tent and the Colonel's tent were among the first to have been set up.

"Somehow, it jest don't seem right t'...."

"Look...if you're so concerned," Obediah said, swinging down from his mount in front of the command post, "you go back and get 'im."

"Well, it's just that...."

"But before you do, see that the horses are cared for first," Obediah said, cutting the man off in mid-sentence and disappearing into the large tent.

Colonel Alexander looked up from a map he had been discussing with another officer, a Captain, whose back was to Obediah as he entered the tent.

"Well?" the Colonel snapped.

"Somebody shot Tatum, but he'll come around in a while."

"Where is he? Did you bring him back?"

"I thought it might aide his recovery if we left 'im out in the fresh air," Obediah said. "When he does come to, he's going to have one powerful headache. Might be best if he worked off some of his meanness finding his way back to camp. He's gonna be one mad he-bear."

"Any idea who did it?" the Captain asked.

"Jones, this is Captain Van Vliet, Quartermaster."

"No...I don't know for sure, Captain," Obediah said, slouching into a camp chair. "But I've got my ideas."

"Are you going to tell us it's the Mormons?" Alexander responded, hotly. "I don't buy your argument that they are already aware of our whereabouts, if that's your answer."

"Well, sir," Obediah said, quietly, "I have no idea who it might have been, except that there were two of them, and that they were riding two well-shod horses, which Indians don't. And, if you'll pardon my saying so, deer don't ride horses and shoot Hawken rifles."

"Now, Jones...."

"Furthermore, Colonel, if you'll pardon the interruption, all the sign indicates that Tatum was setting up an ambush, but it looks like two very savvy characters turned the tables on him. You can explain it anyway you want to, but who would Tatum be laying for when he's got a whole army to back him up?"

"Well...somehow I find it difficult to accept the idea that we're already under enemy observation."

"This isn't my argument, Colonel," Captain Van Vliet interjected, "but given the situation, prudence would argue that even if we have no hard evidence, we should assume a worse-case situation."

"Of course, you're correct, Captain," the Colonel said. Thoroughly irritated, he turned to the map on the table. "And that makes your mission all the more important."

"I quite agree, sir."

"Look here, Jones," Alexander said, motioning the scout to the table. "It's imperative that Captain Van Vliet be taken as quickly as possible into the Mormon city."

"Into the...."

"That's right. It is his mission to scout the trail for forage and fuel between here and the Great Basin, and then he is to negotiate...."

The Colonel stopped in mid-sentence, eyed Obediah Jones carefully, and said, "You understand that this is to be kept in the utmost confidence, Mr. Jones." It was a statement of fact, not a question.

"I've yet to ever betray a confidence," Obediah

responded, "and I don't...."

"It's just that we have to be very careful, Mr. Jones," Captain Van Vliet quickly responded, sensing Obediah's irritation.

"No problem here, Captain. I understand...it's been a long day, hasn't it?"

"Indeed it has, Mr. Jones. My apologies, and please be assured that I do not doubt you," Alexander said, slumping into a camp chair on the opposite side of the small table.

"At any rate, Captain Van Vliet is to attempt to negotiate with Brigham Young for a peaceful entry of this command into Great Salt Lake City," Alexander said, leaning across the map, the exhaustion of the day showing in his face. "I only hope they will listen to reason."

The three men studied the map in silence, each hoping the coming conflict could be somehow avoided. Each knew that the position of the Mormons appeared hopeless, but that they would undoubtedly do all that they felt was necessary to protect themselves. Each also knew that with the commitment of so many men at such great expense, no government could afford to fail in such an effort—the entire operation was simply too controversial to risk failure.

All of the elements of a bloody conflict were present: a unified people with their backs to the wall, an invading (or peace-keeping, depending on one's point of view) army, and an equal degree of dogged determination on each side.

Captain Van Vliet turned from the table and looked directly at Obediah Jones. "Well, what do you think?"

"Anything's worth a try, Captain."

"But, what chance of success?"

* * *

The wind slapped at Jasper's face with a chilling intensity that forebode the onset of an early winter, and the quakies in the high country fluttered a bright yellow in the chilled air. From the blackness below, the fires of Colonel Alexander's advanced units blinked back at the mountain man as he crouched in the brush at the edge of the bluff.

Porter Rockwell dropped beside him with a quiet thud. "Another day's push t' Fort Laramie, an' it already feels like winter's comin'."

"Yep," Jasper grunted, "nearly the middla September and I'm feelin' it a'ready."

"Ain't long b'fore them fools's gonna be hurtin'."

"'Fraid so," Jasper agreed. "Some choice...face us Mormons...," Jasper cleared his throat, "you Mormons an' me ahead of 'em, or turn tail and ma'be face winter an' starvation on the great plains behind 'em." Jasper lay quiet for a moment, and then said, "Seems t' me that'd be the smarter of the two."

"What's that?"

"Turn tale and skedaddle."

Rockwell chuckled, "Yeah...some choice. They ain't really int' the mountains yet, and I'll bet not a mother's son of 'em knows the country twixt here and the Great Salt Lake Valley worth a damn."

"It's cold...let's move," Jasper said, crawling from the edge of the bluff. "Either one of us knows 'em like the backs of our hands—ten years of knowin'."

"It gives us the kind of odds I purely favor," Rockwell snickered, shaking the weeds and dirt from his clothes.

"Damned tomfoolery," Jasper grumbled to himself.

"If I had my way, I'd skin every last man among 'em an'

leave their stinkin' carcasses fer the buzzards."

"We need t' get back and report on this bunch," Jasper said, quickening his pace through the dark trees.

"Not s' fast, Pughsey," Porter Rockwell said, grabbing Jasper by the arm. "I say we sneak down there and stampede their cattle right through that camp."

Jasper Pughsey stopped cold and jerked his arm away from Rockwell's grasp. The men stood close together, but neither could see more than the outline of the other in the cold darkness. Jasper took a deep breath to control his rising temper and said, "We both got our orders, Rockwell. We don't do nothin' t' start trouble 'til we're told."

"Pughsey, you...."

"I don't know what you think you are, but I'm only a scout. And right now, thet's all I'm gonna do. Like it 'r no."

"Well...you may as well know right now...scout," the bearded man said with irritating emphasis, "I ain't s' particular. Everything they get, they'll surely earn, an' just bein' here, they've earned some."

"There's good men down there," Jasper said, moving on into the darkness. "Surely they ain't all bad. Some of 'em...."

"So that's it," Rockwell said bitterly, "maybe yer faverin' 'em some, huh?"

Jasper refused to answer the bitter charge, afraid of what his response might be. He respected this dark, unshorn man, and he liked the mystery that seemed to be a part of Rockwell's almost obsessive commitment, but Jasper wanted no argument with him. Things were getting too hot between them in the cold night air.

The surrounding hills were dotted with juniper, pinon, and sagebrush, and the two men had earlier built a sparse lean-to in a shallow draw some distance from the army encampment.

After encouraging a small fire, the two settled down in stubborn silence to a scant meal of canned beans and what remained of a cold night, each filled with his own growing resentment.

Beneath the heavy, black brows, the almost unnaturally pale eyes sparked from the fire light as Porter Rockwell looked at Jasper and said, "What I said back there, Pughsey...well...I never meant it."

"Ferget it," Jasper said, his voice soft in the night. "Things is tense, I know thet."

"Yeah...but Pughsey...there's somethin' you need t' understand about me."

"An what might thet be?"

"There's two men I'd walk into hell with and whitewash it...Joseph Smith and Brigham Young." Rockwell spat into the fire and looked thoughtfully at Jasper Pughsey. "I almost did with Joseph, and I surely may have to with Brother Brigham...and by the Eternal, if it has 't be done, I'll do it."

"I know...I heard all the stories."

"Well...that's how come I don't take pleasantly t' soft talk about them heathen back there. Every man jack of 'em deserves 'is misery. And if I can do any thing t' add to it, I surely will." Taking a deep breath, Rockwell continued, "Me 'an my people don't never inflict misery on anyone...least ways the Church surely don't. We take more'n we give, by a damn sight. But one thing you 'an me need t' get straight between us...ain't no army of any description or size comin' into these mountains and drivin' us out. As long as I got breath, we ain't goin' t' know another Nauvoo."

Orrin Porter Rockwell poked at the dying fire with a stick and said, "Question is where d' you stand?"

"I'm here, ain't I?" Jasper responded, his irritation rising again.

"I figgered as much."

"Don't know why, though."

"Maybe, after all these years you been tellin' me about, somethin's eatin' at ya," Rockwell said. "Somethin' y' ain't willin' t' admit t' yerself, let alone t' me."

"Thet's a lot a foofuraw. Bunch a pork eaters out here on the frontier..."

"Pork eaters, y' say?" Rockwell responded, looking hard at Jasper Pughsey. "Us pork eaters ain't exactly goin' under, now, are we? Brother Brigham's moved folks all over. How far can you ride without runnin' on t' a Mormon settlement? Answer me that! And in only ten years, t' boot.... Oh, we're here alright. Ain't nothin' gonna change that fact."

"Yeah...an' when all's said an' done, thet ain't all so good. Yew ever stop t' think of that?"

"Well, fer all yer complainin', I can't help but notice you still hang around these parts a whole lot. An', as a matter of fact, as reluctant as y' seem, here ya are with me t'night arguin' yer head off about ya don't know what, an' enjoyin' a hard bed in the great outta doors. What I'd like t' know is, how come?"

"Thet's exactly what I mean," Jasper shot back. "Look't all these white people out here runnin' around buildin' towns an' such. How they gonna survive out here? Ain't no food t' speak of an' precious little water t' grow it with—if the land'd grow anything but sage and salt grass."

"Well, now maybe you ain't noticed, but we seem t' be doin' well enough on what we are," Rockwell said, his voice growing low. "An' fer all yer fuss, you still ain't answered why yer hangin' around these parts if yer so against our bein' here."

His anger growing from Rockwell's persistence, Jasper said, "Well, now maybe yew ain't noticed, but if all yew Mormons hadn'ta come out here t' start with, none of this dust-up would've happened, anyways. All y've managed t' do is upset the Injuns an' bring all these pony soldiers out here where they don't belong neither."

"Unlike us, they ain't gonna be here that long...."

"Ma'be, ma'be not, thet...."

"Now just whaddaya mean by that, Pughsey?"

"I mean them what belongs here is Elk, and Timponogos, an' their folks. They's wild an' free an' belong t' the land as it is, not as they suppose it oughta be."

"Well, now I jest can't help but notice that you're out here, and you're white. You took your share of beaver, and y' don't exactly blend in none. That can't be none too pleasin' t' them Lamanites, neither."

"Them what?"

"Them...redskins."

"Well, I'm a darn sight more like 'em than yew folks, now ain't I?"

"Maybe that's yer problem. You...."

"I'm what," Jasper shot back, his voice rising in anger.

"You ain't neither. Yer not one of them and yer not one of us...or are ya?"

Jasper jumped to his feet and threw his bean can into the fire, scattering embers. "I'll tell ya what I am, I'm gone, thet's what I am."

"Ain't nothin' stoppin' us, Pughsey. You'd better get it straight, and make up yer mind."

"It's made up. I'm...."

"You'll be back Pughsey. Yer one of us," Rockwell shouted as Jasper's form melted into the blackness of the surrounding brush. "Ya can't run from it Pughsey. Yer one of us. You just haven't come to it yet."

"Yell a little louder, ya fool, an' yew'll have Benko Tatum and that army ya hate s' much up here," Jasper shot back, his voice receding into the darkness.

CHAPTER SIX

From its wide, flat eastern end, Echo Canyon sloped harmlessly off into the dusk of late evening, the increasing darkness denying the two riders more than a hint of the massive, geological fortifications that lay below them in the distance. It had been nearly ten years since Obediah last saw the canyon, but he had no difficulty remembering what lay before them.

Captain Stewart Van Vliet leaned forward in his saddle and studied the canyon with the look of a man who performed his duties with true military prudence. He was a career army officer, a graduate of West Point, and a man given to careful forethought and circumspection, undoubtedly one reason why a company-grade officer of the Quartermaster Corps had been selected months before by General William S. Harney himself for such an important and delicate mission.

Though he was charged with determining what forage and fuel was available between South Pass and Great Salt Lake City, the young captain's primary mission was to meet with Mormon leaders and report back to his military commanders the likelihood of serious opposition.

The horses stomped and blew impatiently as their two riders surveyed the darkening canyon below them.

"Don't let it fool you," Obediah Jones said. "It deepens and narrows before you get to the end."

"Rather like a funnel, would you say?" Van Vliet said, settling back in his saddle.

"Dangerously so. At the bottom you will be hemmed in

by cliffs on each side and in front of you. It is a natural
choke point," Obediah said, dismounting. "As you'll see
tomorrow, forage is not your problem."

"Well...you're our scout, Mr. Jones," Van Vliet said, as
he dismounted and followed Obediah to a large stand of fir
and Quaking Aspen. "What do you suggest?"

"Its not my responsibility to suggest. I just scout,"
Obediah said, tying his horse to a small tree. "Let's gather
some dry fuel. I could use some warmth and some hot
coffee."

"Well...I know the limitations of your duties, man, but
if...."

"I can only tell you this, Captain," Obediah said,
stopping to look squarely at Van Vliet, "if Brigham Young
doesn't want your army to enter the Salt Lake Valley, right
down there is where it will be stopped," he said, nodding
toward the canyon. "A handful of determined men could
slaughter the entire command."

Stacking the dry branches carefully, Obediah soon had
a small, but enthusiastic fire crackling with hot efficiency.
What little smoke it produced was effectively dissipated
among the aspen leaves above the two men.

Taking a battered, blackened coffee pot from a saddle
bag, Obediah looked at Van Vliet and said, "And if there is
one thing I know about the Mormons, they are determined."

Van Vliet settled himself a few feet from the fire and
gazed into it thoughtfully. "I'm afraid your assessment of
both the situation and the Mormons is accurate, Mr. Jones.
I've dealt with them before, too. They are a people of
determination and great faith. Believe me, I do not
underestimate them."

"Well...I'm not so sure the same can be said for some of

the others involved in this exercise."

"Perhaps you're right. That's why I'm grateful for your assistance in getting me through these endless mountains. I hope I can bring both sides to some accommodation and prevent unnecessary bloodshed."

"Well...Alexander's army is going to need more than forage."

"I'm looking for peace, Jones. What's happening is more a consequence of bigotry and misunderstanding than anything else. As things are now, nobody wins."

"True as that is, I wish you success Captain, because if the Mormons decide to fight, your troops will never reach the end of this canyon. It'll be a blood bath, and there's really no other way into the Great Basin from here—at least one that you can traverse in a matter of days."

Wrapping his hand with a large handkerchief, Obediah removed the bubbling pot from the fire, poured the hot coffee into two tin cups, and settled next to Van Vliet. The steaming, black liquid warmed both men, tired from a long day's ride.

Obediah stirred his coffee with a small twig, and said, "This whole thing strikes me as little more than a big political boondoggle, Captain." Staring reflectively into the swirling, black liquid, he continued, "These people have done nothing that deserves this kind of treatment. Near as I can tell, all they've ever wanted is to live their religion."

"Mm...unfortunately, you're probably right."

"How come that's so bothersome to so many people— bothersome enough to send an army?" Obediah asked, looking squarely at Van Vliet. "To do what? Subdue them? Wipe them out?"

"I don't know, frankly," Van Vliet responded with a sigh.

"I'm a soldier. I follow orders," he continued, staring into the slowly, dying fire.

"You think that's good enough?"

Van Vliet poured himself more coffee, and asked, "What's your interest in these people, anyway? You seem to know a good deal about them."

"I've spent years trapping these mountains from south of here clear up to the Bitterroot country. I guess I know them about as well as any man—with the possible exception of Jasper Pughsey; he was my partner most of the time."

The fire hissed as Obediah threw the remains of his cup into the hot coals, and continued, "At any rate, Jasper and I were planning on spending the winter of '47 hitting the towns along the Mississippi, living it up for a change. We'd had a few good years and had a few coins in our britches. But out on the prairie, way late in the season, as I recall, we met these three Mormon kids trying to get to the Great Basin on their own."

"How old were they? Were they lost?"

"Just youngsters, in their teens. But the boy...oh, I don't know, barely ten or twelve, I guess. That kid had more whistle in his britches than most men I know, and he was determined to get his sisters safely out with their people."

"Where were their parents?"

"Dead. Killed when Nauvoo was sacked and burned."

"I take it you got them there."

"Oh, yeah. Between the two of us, we got them there," the scout said, rising from his place by the fire. "And that's what makes me so all-fired uncomfortable about this whole thing you and I are caught up in."

"How's that?" Van Vliet asked, looking up at the scout.

"Just seems like more of the same. Is it ever going to end for them?"

"That's why I've got to do what I've got to do, and why your help is so important, Mr. Jones," Van Vliet said. "When are we likely to arrive in Great Salt Lake?"

"We'll push hard, and if those fellas down there below us let us through, we should get there in a couple of days."

"Down where? You mean in the canyon, there?"

"That's what I mean."

"But...how in the world...?"

"I know you already know it, Captain, but its not wise to look directly into the fire. Let your eyes get used to the dark, and you'll see two or three fires way off there in the distance."

"Will they stop us in the canyon?"

"I don't think so. Judging from their fires, they're up on the canyon's rims—right where you'd expect them. Besides, the only thing threatening about us is your uniform. I think they'll let us through, but we'll be watched until you get into Salt Lake."

"I hope there'll be no violence."

"Hasn't been so far, except for the crease in Benko Tatum's worthless scalp the other day."

"The man's lucky he wasn't killed."

"Tatum manages to create his own luck, one way or the other," Obediah said, spitting the last mouthful of coffee and grounds into the fire. "But luck had nothing to do with it. Whoever shot Benko Tatum did not intend to kill him, just put him down for a while—for an up-close inspection, judging from the sign." Obediah paused, looking off into the darkness that covered their small camp. "Had a kind of a familiar look to it, too."

The soldier threw his blanket on the ground and settled down a few feet a way, staring at the glimmering brilliance of the mountain sky through the black shadows of the leaves above him. "How's that?"

"Oh...it looked like Tatum was setting up some sort of ambush. That in itself looked familiar, but it was the sign left by the other two—I don't know.

"I don't like to say this of any human being, Mr. Jones, but I intensely dislike the man."

"Don't feel too badly, Captain Van Vliet," Obediah said, rolling himself into his blanket. "I don't know anyone who doesn't."

"You seem to know him fairly well."

"I don't know if I could say that I know 'im, but I've had more than one run-in with him. What I do know about him is that you don't cross him and then turn your back on him."

"I know this sounds odd, but he reminds me of a snake."

"He is a snake, and you don't want to trust him any further than you would a snake. More than once he nearly got me and my partner killed."

"Your partner?"

"Yep," Obediah said, trying to settle his body around the lumpy ground beneath him. "Old Jasper Pughsey and I did a lot of trapping a few years ba...wait a minute!" Obediah Jones said, bolting upright. "That's it," he said, slapping his leg.

"What's wrong, Mr. Jones?" Captain Van Vliet said, sitting up with some alarm. "What is it?"

"That sign around Tatum when he got shot. It was Jasper Pughsey that shot 'im. I'd stake my last plew on it—

that's what I recognized. I know how that old beaver's stick floats, and now I really think about it, that crease in Benko Tatum's head had Jasper Pughsey written all over it."

Jasper Pughsey angrily threw his saddle on his horse. Rockwell's nosey accusations rang in his ears, and thunder could be heard in the distance.

For all of that, what was he doing here, anyway, Jasper wondered. *Who are these Mormons, and why the devil am I helpin' 'em? Things ain't been right since I got tangled up with 'em ten years ago. They ain't my people, ain't none of my business. Was I one of 'em?* he thought, bitterly. *What business is it of that long-haired, whisker-faced pilgrim, anyways?*

"Bunch a pork eaters," he mumbled aloud, as he mounted his horse and urged it into the dark, cold night. The wind was rising, and occasional lightning flashed in the distance giving sudden but abrupt relief to the almost total darkness.

Jasper Pughsey had always been a man of action, reacting to each situation as it arose. He was a survivor, and he had survived for many years in the wild mountains of the west, not because he philosophized about the whys of things, but because he reacted to the imperatives of things as he found them—or they found him. He had the scars of experience, but no one or no thing had put him under. He had survived, and that was enough.

In the wild, that's how you had to be, Jasper thought. *Too much thinkin' ain't good fer a man's future. While he's sittin' around contemplatin', a man can lose 'is hair.*

"Thet coon Rockwell," Jasper spoke to his horse. "Who's

'e think 'e is, anyways, askin' all them fool questions? Questionin' my loyalty like 'e did. Wagh!"

The lightning imperceptibly but steadily became more frequent, and from each sudden flash, the deep, almost languid, thunder rolled closer.

Thet ain't how it is, he thought. *I know dern well who I am. I ain't tied down t' nothin' 'r nobody, that's what. I'm part of this wild country, an' all of these fools, army and Mormons alike, ain't a part of it.*

The cold wind blew more persistently in Jasper's face with gusts that had begun to have a chilling sting to them. *Still...Rockwell's got a point. What's these folks done t' deserve an army comin' out here t' crush 'em?*

"Ones I know're all good folks," Jasper mumbled to the horse.

Large rain drops spattered across him, and a smile creased the mountain man's face as he remembered Butch and his sisters, the adventures they all had as he and Obediah got them across the plains and through the mountains to Great Salt Lake City.

"Good folks," he said aloud. The old trapper's heart warmed whenever he thought of Butch and the girls.

Jasper's thoughts were interrupted as a bolt of lightning split the dark night with sudden brilliance, and a clap of thunder rolled off into the night. But the stillness that remained was broken with the sound of nervous cattle somewhere ahead in the darkness. Urging his horse cautiously forward, Jasper rode out onto a rocky promontory. Back to his left he could see the dying fires of the army encampment, and directly below him in the dark were the cattle and horses of the invading army.

Tying his horse to a tree well back from the cliff, Jasper

moved cautiously out to the edge of the rim rock. Though the night was dark with the intensifying storm, the increasing flashes of lightning enabled him to make out what seemed to be a substantial herd of beef cattle nervously milling about in a shallow box canyon below him. There were more than he had thought, judging from the trail he and Porter Rockwell had been following.

Enough meat there t' keep these troopers through the winter, he thought, *eatin' real well, too. They could wait and move on the Mormons next spring if they were of mind to.* Jasper scratched his head. *Thet might just be their sneaky plan.*

"Best I get back t' Port Rockwell," Jasper mumbled to himself, "and tell...." But another thought overwhelmed him: *thet much beef on the hoof could surely upset a sleeping camp and ruin a night's rest fer them army pork eaters.*

"I'll show thet coon Rockwell, who's who around here," he muttered to himself, edging away from the cliff.

A cold shower of rain spattered across the rock and through the brush and trees as the mountain man followed the ragged edge of the small box canyon to a point near its mouth where a rock-fall sloped to the bottom. A flash of lightning caused the wet rock below him to glisten and become lost in the darkness.

Cautiously, Jasper climbed down the inside edge of the rock-fall and lowered himself silently from a large bolder to the ground, careful not to spook the increasingly restless cattle. Moving quietly through the herd, he located two guards near the mouth of the canyon, not far from where he had descended from the rim. One sat slumped against a large rock apparently asleep, the other pacing back and forth watching the milling herd with increasing apprehension. A large number of horses were in a makeshift pole corral just outside the mouth of the canyon, separate from the cattle.

The flimsy gate enclosing the cattle amounted to nothing more than three long poles cut from sapling pine trees and laid one above the other across the small opening to the rocky, enclosed canyon. Each pole had been jammed between large rocks on each side of the canyon's mouth, but it was obvious to Jasper that the least pressure would cause the fragile barrier to break loose, freeing the cattle.

The rain, though still light, was becoming steady and the lightning and thunder more frequent, persistent, and annoying. Jasper Pughsey made his way through the cattle and horses to the opposite end of the canyon where the rock walls on each side gave way to a steep pine- and juniper-covered slope that reached the shallow canyon's rim.

Easy pickin's, Jasper thought to himself, as he made his way back to his horse. *I'll show thet Orrin Porter Rockwell who's the smart coyote.* His cold fingers fumbled with the wet reins and climbing aboard the skittish animal, he said, "This child don't need that bristly-faced critter. You an' me's gonna throw a party. An' Rockwell can jest set and watch. Come on...get!"

Newly promoted Sergeant Major Timothious James O'Riley's tent was properly pitched at the end of two rows of smartly dressed military tents where his men were bedded down after a long, dusty day on the trail. Along each row, not a tent, rope, or peg was out of line, each resembling the other in its place and in proper military detail.

To Sergeant Major O'Riley, the difficulty of the day did not interfere with Army discipline, at war, at rest, or on the trail. Before one of his men could call it a day, things would be in their proper place and smartly set. Such discipline, however, was amply punctuated with the big Irishman's good nature, his motherly concern for the welfare of his blue-clad charges, and generous helpings of liquid spirits, if and when available.

It was O'Riley's eye to detail, and the esteem and affection with which he was held by enlisted men and officers alike, that caused Colonel Alexander to choose him as his Top Sergeant, despite the Sergeant's occasional lapses into intemperance—a weakness of his Irish flesh that caused him no end of remorse and histrionic self-reproach, particularly when under the influence.

The Sergeant resembled a large hibernating bear as he lay in his tent, curled beneath his blanket. The standard army issue blanket rose and fell with each even breath, but every flash of lightning and clap of thunder caused his eyelids to flutter and his brow to furrow more deeply.

Large drops of rain thumped irritatingly across the heavy canvas, and the night exploded as a bolt of lightning split a nearby tree somewhere on the bluff above the encampment, momentarily lighting the tent's interior. The resounding peal of thunder sat Sergeant O'Riley upright in his bed, a heavy, disquieting rumble growing from its dying reverberations.

Though cold, the air in the small tent was damp and close, and O'Riley strained momentarily to recognize the on-coming rumble as the ground beneath him began to vibrate.

"Holy Mother of...not the cattle...."

Stumbling barefoot out into the now pelting rain, the

Sergeant struggled to get his pants up as he thumbed his wide suspenders over each shoulder, his long red underwear plastered to his body by the force of the downpour.

With an almost blinding flash of lightning, the tidy military scene of the evening before appeared to explode into the chaos of a battlefield. The beef herd charged through the encampment, scattering men in every direction from the splintering, shredding line of tents.

To O'Riley, it was like a bad dream, the frequent lightning strikes seeming to stop everything in unsteady, terrifying jerks, and in the middle of the maelstrom of rain, hoofs, and lightning thundering down upon him was a wild, screaming face—a wild-eyed face that froze in the Top Sergeant's memory as he ran for the cover of large rocks at the base of the nearby bluffs.

It was over as suddenly as it had begun, and as the herd stampeded around the bluffs and out onto the dark prairie, the rain stopped and a cold, steady wind began to part the clouds, allowing a large, full moon to provide some relief from the almost total darkness.

"Corporal of the Guard!" O'Riley hollered, as he walked through the shattered remains of the camp toward the group of highly agitated officers that had crowded around their commanding officer. O'Riley forced himself to stifle a chuckle at the sight of his superiors, all appearing militarily equal in their unmilitarily soggy, long underwear.

Colonel Alexander pushed the men aside and looked at his Sergeant Major, a smile crossing his tired face. "Sergeant you're out of uniform."

"Indeed I am, sir. And a most unpleasant feelin' it is, too, if I do say so meself, sir."

"Indeed it is, Top. Let's get the men assembled quickly. We need to round up as many horses as possible. I think we've had our first visit from the Mormons."

Turning to his officers, Alexander said, "Anyone know if Jones has returned from...."

"Sir," one of the officers said looking into the night where the herd had disappeared, "it may not be over."

Urging his horse to the front of the charging cattle, Jasper Pughsey began forcing the leading animals into a tight turn and the stampede began to collapse into a milling, agitated herd.

Reloading his revolver, and firing it repeatedly into the air, Jasper hollered, "One more time...jest so's them pony soldiers know we was here."

The shots and screams in their midst soon had the frightened, restless cattle moving in a headlong charge back in the direction from which they had just come, filling the predawn air with a muddy spray and chunks of wet earth and loose rock. With the herd rumbling into the already shattered encampment and on toward the supply wagons, Jasper began reining in his horse in an effort to leave the stampede to its destructive work while he made his escape.

As the herd thundered from around him, Jasper Pughsey was suddenly and cruelly yanked from his saddle, the rude rope around his arms and chest squeezing the air from his lungs, slamming into the ground, and snapping him violently into the mud.

* * *

Black melted into gray and unwillingly Jasper Pughsey began to make out shapes above him in the slowly brightening light. His head ached, and his chest felt as though he had been repeatedly kicked by a mule. Everything he had hurt. Through the haze, the shapes began to form into heads and then heads with discernible features. Recognizing one of the faces, the mountain man longed for the darkness to return.

Benko Tatum leaned down into his old enemy's face. "Jasper Pughsey, you dumb coon. How'd you think you could get away with what you done?" he said, jabbing Jasper viciously in the ribs. "Huh?"

Jasper's hand reflexively shot up grabbing Tatum's shirt, but Tatum jabbed him again, and a wave of nausea weld up. Darkness again swept over the mountain man.

O'Riley grabbed Tatum by the collar and yanked him away from the unconscious man, shoving him to the rear of the tent. "So, it's a fight ya want now, is it?" he said, a nasty grin splitting his reddening face.

Tatum backed away, eyes darting between the big Sergeant and the man lying on the cot. "Best you stay outta this, O'Riley. He's mine, an' you ain't got no say in it. I'm the one what brought 'im down."

"That you did, lad. That you did," the Sergeant said, giving Tatum a nasty shove in the chest, causing the scout to lose his balance and fall to the dirt floor of the large tent. "But he now belongs t' the United States Army and not t' the likes a you. Now, lad," O'Riley said, to Tatum, as he turned back to Jasper Pughsey, "be about yer business, and trouble me no more. Y've hovered over this poor lad like a fly fer most of a day, now. Me patience has come to a end."

The Sergeant Major leaned over and squinted into Jasper's face. "What this fine fellow needs is a wee bit of stimulant t' bring 'im about is all," he said, pulling a flat, brown bottle of whisky from his hip pocket and taking a generous gulp. "Jest what 'e needs t' take some of the harshness away from it all."

Tatum's hand felt the cool handle of the knife in its scabbard at the small of his back. "I ain't one a yer blue-bellied tin soldiers dancin' t' yer tune, O'Riley," he said, the knife sliding from its hiding place. "I aim t' finish 'im one way or the other."

Thinking the large Irishman an easy target, Tatum jabbed with the knife from a squatting position, but he was too slow. With the sudden movement behind him, O'Riley ducked, whirling around blocking the thrust with one arm and swinging his precious bottle in an arc that caught the stunned scout squarely in the side of his face, shattering the bottle and splashing its treasured contents across the canvas wall of the tent.

Blood spattered from Benko Tatum's nose, and the scout suddenly and painfully found himself bouncing off the bulging tent wall, and back into an on-coming fist that caught him squarely in his belly. The big Sergeant came up into Benko Tatum's face with a wicked right that straightened him up and slammed him on his back in the dirt, out cold.

Jasper Pughsey gradually sat up swinging his leaden feet to the floor. "Thet was about as purty a sight as I've ever seen," he said, resting his aching head in his hands.

"It was, indeed, and at great personal loss t' the both of us," O'Riley said, viewing the shattered bottle of whisky mournfully. "What has been lost this day cannot be easily replaced in this unholy place."

The Sergeant reached down and picked up Tatum's knife, examining it with a critical eye. "But y' must understand that it's a true man of peace that I am, there bein' not a violent bone in me body. But there's them amongst us that tests even the most perserverin'. Still, 'tis filled with proper Christian charity that I am fer Mr. Tatum, here," he said, giving the inert body a sharp jab with the toe of his boot. "Poor motherless child that 'e was."

"Poor motherless child?" Jasper repeated with wonder, momentarily forgetting his pain. "Well, now, jest let me tell...."

"But with the likes a you...destroyin' gover'ment property an' all as y' done...there's always the end of a rope."

"Thet's yer Christian charity? An' y'll let him go, huh?"

"Well now, lad, let's just look at things as they appear t' be," the Sergeant offered, a deceptively friendly smile splitting his large, red face. "Was it you who was caught destroyin' our peaceful camp, was it? And was it you who stampeded our cattle, scatterin' our horses an' all, was it? And while we was properly asleep, was it? And during the nastiest of storms, was it? And was it you whose miserable and traitorous acts cost me an' these good men two whole days an' more gatherin' up what's rightfully ours, was it? And us s' far from home, too. And was it that poor lad there," he asked, jerking his large, stubby thumb toward Benko Tatum, now beginning to stir, "who caught ya red-handed at yer nasty business, was it? An' me all wet and soaked in the rain in me underwear."

Reaching over and poking Jasper's shoulder, he said, "Lucky fer you nobody was hurt. At least now it's a fair trial you'll be gettin'. Then we'll hang ya, lad. All nice an' tidy."

"Hang me?" Jasper said, trying to rise.

"Hang ya," O'Riley said, shoving him back onto the cot.

"But all I done was move yer cattle some fer ya. Thet ain't no hangin' offense!"

"Well, now," the Sergeant said, easing his bulk onto the cot next to Jasper, "under these tryin' conditions of movin' an army an all, I'm at a loss as t' what t' do with ya. Hangin' seems the most practical solution. An' that's not even takin' int' account the unfortunate loss of me last bottle of comfort."

"Well...I'll jest warn ya right now," Jasper said, rubbing his sore, aching back, "I jest might not be as easy t' hang as yew seem t' think."

Getting up from the low cot, O'Riley frowned down on the mountain man. "I'll listen t' no more threats from the likes a you."

"Well...but you...."

"Harris!" the Sergeant yelled at the guard outside the tent. "Get poor old Tatum outta here, lest we have more trouble."

Pulling back the heavy canvas flap as Tatum's semiconscious body was unceremoniously drug from the tent, O'Riley said, "Still 'tis admiration I've got fer someone such as yerself. A proper hangin'd be too bothersome fer all concerned—fer the time bein', anyway."

"Well...now...jest...."

"I'll just be thinkin' of somethin' even better," the Sergeant said, as the tent flap dropped behind him, leaving Jasper Pughsey to face his aches and pains alone.

* * *

Two days later, Jasper Pughsey sat dejectedly atop his horse, his hands bound tightly behind him, and moodily watched the confusion of an army breaking camp. His raid on their bivouac and the damage done by the stampede had cost the invading army dearly in time, equipment, and animals. The loss of each day became even more critical as the season grew late.

He had done exactly what was expected of him, and at great cost to the invading army. Some of the damage was beyond repair. A number of tents had been shredded beneath the charging hoofs, several wagons had been badly damaged and taken precious time to repair, their contents ruined in the rain and mud. In addition, a large number of horses had gotten caught up in the stampede and were never found. But just as he and Rockwell had been instructed, no one was killed—a few sore bodies and broken limbs, but no loss of life. In fact, the more Jasper thought about it, the more his spirits lifted. *Small wonder O'Riley was talkin' about a hangin'*, he thought.

Just as the mountain man was beginning to feel better, Benko Tatum walked out of a nearby tent, mounted his horse, and reined up next to Jasper. He was obviously in an ugly mood, his face swollen and scabbed where O'Riley's bottle had broken, and a nasty bruise ran from the corner of his mouth along his jaw, not to mention the neat crease in his scalp earlier made by Jasper's Hawken. Though he had his suspicions, Tatum was still uncertain of the author of that indignity.

Tatum spat a wad on the ground between their two mounts, barely missing Jasper's horse. "You dumb coon," he growled, his face twisted with hatred. "Yer a dead man,

Pughsey. You ain't goin' t' live t' see the sun set if'n I get my way."

Caught on top of a horse with his hands tied behind his back, the mountain man struggled against an unfamiliar feeling of helplessness. The two had been natural enemies from the beginning, and over the years the mere sight of the hairless trapper filled Jasper Pughsey with contempt, and it was obvious in the tone of his voice.

"And jest how d' you figger t' pull thet off?" he asked, straightening himself in the saddle in an attempt to overcome the uncomfortable feeling of vulnerability. "Yew don't know poor bull from fat cow. Wagh."

"No more, Pughsey. Yer goin' under b'fore this day's over."

"Not by your hand," Jasper spat. "All I seen so far of you is you on yer scabby backside in the dirt. And if my hands weren't tied behind me, this child'd lay ya there again. Wagh!"

Jasper's foot suddenly flew out and caught Tatum's horse squarely in its flank, sending the startled animal into a bucking melee that caught Tatum completely off guard and ended with him on his back in the dirt.

The dazed scout struggled to his feet, but laughter from several troopers who witnessed the sudden action prevented him from drawing his knife and killing Jasper Pughsey on the spot.

"I'll get you Pughsey. I'll get you, if it's the last thing I ever do," the enraged man hissed, keeping his voice low. "Before this day is done, I'm gonna...."

"I know how yer stick floats, yew smelly polecat. The only way you'll put this child under is if I'm tied hand and foot," Jasper spat. "Yew ain't man enough t' do it elsewise."

Benko Tatum slowly brushed the dirt from his buckskin pants and moved up next to Jasper's horse, obscuring the view of the troopers working around them. "This is only a taste of what's t' come...coon," he said.

Jasper Pughsey winced from the painful bite of Tatum's knife, as the humiliated scout viciously sliced a deep gash in Jasper's leg.

"Next time it'll be yer belly I open up, Pughsey," he hissed, as he turned and stalked off to find his horse.

The flap of the command tent slapped the side of the tent as Sergeant Major O'Riley emerged and walked over to Pughsey.

"Well, lad, we must put off yer hangin' until we've more time t' enjoy it proper-like, and so I've...what've ya done t' yer leg, man? Yer bleedin' like Mrs. Murphy's goat."

"It ain't nothin'. Reckon I drug it again' a nail, what with m'hands tied an' all."

"A nail...where...?"

"Jest one a them things, I guess," Jasper responded, irritably. "Now, let's jest...."

"Well...we'll see to it, man," O'Riley said, admiring the bloody gash in Jasper's pants more closely, "an' then I'm havin' Tatum take ya on t' Fort Bridger."

"Fort Bridger?" Jasper responded, trying to keep a grin from splitting his face. "Y' don't say?"

"Oh, I do indeed, lad. It'll be more accommodatin' for us all. You'll be all nice'n snug waitin' fer us t' bring the rope, and we'll be free of the likes of you...at least fer a while."

The mountain man could hardly believe his ears. How could Colonel Alexander not know that Fort Bridger had become a Mormon outpost and settlement? It was the least likely place for the army to find any kind of assistance, let alone imprison one of Rockwell's scouts.

All I gotta do, he chuckled to himself, *is survive long enough t' ride int' Fort Bridger, an' I'll be right back out the next day makin' life miser'ble fer O'Riley and his blue-bellies all over again.*

His biggest worry was keeping Tatum from carrying out his threats long enough to get to Fort Bridger. If Jasper could do that, he was a free man.

"Now...lookie here, blue-belly," Jasper said, leaning over and staring O'Riley straight in his large, red face. "If yew really want t' see me dancin' at the end of a rope, yew better have somebody between me an' Benko Tatum between now an' then, or y'll have t' make other arrangements."

"Well, now...is that a fact, is it?"

"Best as I knowd how t' tell it."

"And just why might that be, lad?"

"'Cause that polecat and me tangle real serious-like if'n we're even in the same county, let alone under the same tree."

O'Riley eyed his prisoner carefully, knowing what the Mormon scout said was true. Though neither he nor his commanding officer had any intention of hanging Jasper Pughsey, all concerned thought it best to keep the man tightly secured, in the dark, and always guessing.

To that end, they had all agreed that the best way to get him out of their way was to send him on to the vicinity of Fort Bridger where, Tatum had assured Colonel Alexander, some of his mountain cronies had established a small, secluded hangout.

The mountain refuge lay approximately five miles north of the fort on Muddy Creek near an abandoned Shoshone camp site. The place had a few small, crude buildings, one of which, Tatum had explained, could serve as a jail—or something like one. Those that hung out there were not friends of the Mormons, nor were they fond of Pughsey.

It was not a difficult decision to make. Jasper Pughsey had already caused the United States government enough trouble and expense. He had to be neutralized, at least until they had the time to figure out what to do with him.

The Top Sergeant scratched his clean-shaven jaw, and said, "Hangin' ya now might be the simplest thing, then?"

"Might jest be."

"Hmm."

Late in the morning, eight long days and seven relatively sleepless nights later, the three tired troopers, assigned the thankless job of escorting Jasper Pughsey to jail, and Benko Tatum, their scout, reined in their horses atop a small hill that overlooked Fort Bridger.

For all the difficulty that had surrounded it over the last ten years, Fort Bridger was little more than a small cluster of log houses set within a newly-built rock wall, the entire compound located between several branches of Black's Fork of the Green River.

Tatum nudged his horse and angled back down the hill in the direction from which they had just come. "It's thisa way, gents," he hollered over his shoulder. "Oughta be there by nightfall."

His hands tied behind him, Jasper Pughsey twisted in the saddle and looked at the fort as it disappeared behind the hill. "Now jest where d'ya think...?"

Tatum reined in his horse and waited until the three grumbling troopers had passed. Nudging the animal alongside Jasper's, he said, "I know what's been goin' through that empty head a your's...you dumb coon."

Leaning closer to the bound mountain man, he sneered, "Here all this time you was thinkin' we was gonna deliver ya into the hands a yer Mormon cronies, huh? Jest how dumb d'ya think we are, huh?"

"Dumb enough," Jasper spat.

So close Jasper could smell his foul breath, Tatum whispered low, "Sa dumb I'm gonna give it t' ya in the lights and dump yer meatbag all over yer feet soon as these blue-bellies'r outta my way. That's how dumb," he hissed.

The lead soldier turned in his saddle and hollered, "The trail forks here...what'd...."

"T' the left...up the hill," Tatum responded, spurring his horse forward.

The shadows of the tall pines surrounding the small clearing had grown long, almost obscuring the three log and mud cabins that composed the hideout. Each structure looked solidly built, though the whole place had a temporary feeling about it. The entire camp was no larger than an acre and thick stands of pine and Quaking Aspen spilled down from the surrounding mountains threatening to invade the small meadow.

"Get down, Pughsey," one of the troopers ordered.

"Here...let me help 'im," Tatum said, pulling Jasper to the ground and shoving him toward a cabin that stood somewhat apart. The door that hung open had a small, barred window, and a larger, barred window could be seen in the back wall. A flimsy-looking wooden staircase on the outside of one wall led to a second floor that seemed to squat like an afterthought under the low, uneven roof.

"Hey...take it easy," one of the soldiers objected.

"You jest mind yer business, blue-belly. This here beaver's my concern, now," Tatum said, shoving the mountain man roughly across the small clearing.

"Tatum...," Jasper said, falling to his knees and struggling to his feet, "you and me's gonna account fer all this one day."

"You ain't gonna live that long, coon," Tatum said, shoving the mountain man again.

As one of the troopers opened the door wider, Tatum jabbed his foot in Jasper's back and shoved him into the dark room, the mountain man sprawling on his belly, his face in the dirt.

"That ain't called for," one of the troopers said, as he stepped in and sliced the bindings that held Jasper's numb hands. As the man retreated, the door slammed shut muffling Tatum's harsh voice, and a bolt slid into place with a finality that left the mountain man alone and empty.

CHAPTER SEVEN

To Obediah Jones and Captain Stewart Van Vliet, the crisp early autumn air felt invigorating, but the late morning chill had an unwelcome edge to it.

"It's going to be an early winter, Captain," Obediah observed. "A little too chilly this early in September."

"Well," Van Vliet said, shifting uneasily in his saddle, "you were right about this infernal canyon. I have no reason to doubt your word about the weather—much as I don't like either." To the young Captain, the sight around them was not a welcome one. The two riders were surrounded on three sides by sheer granite escarpments that rose precipitously from the canyon floor. Echo Canyon ended abruptly before them, forming the confluence of not one, but three canyons: Echo Canyon gently climbing back the way they had come, the other off to the northwest, and the third leading south and then west through the mountains to Great Salt Lake City. The natural junction before them was not especially narrow, given the depth of the canyon, but anyone holding the canyon's rims could control all movement below with deadly authority—an invading commander's tactical nightmare.

Especially unwelcome was the dark bearded figure that emerged from the trees and willows lining the stream at the far side of the canyon. Spurring his horse, the stranger approached Obediah and Van Vliet at a gentle cantor, his large-bore rifle resting easily across his saddle horn in the general direction of their bellies.

Obediah stiffened slightly in his saddle and said, "I don't

think we should do anything to alarm this gent."

"Good thought, Mr. Jones," Van Vliet replied, chuckling at the irony of Obediah's words.

The stranger rode to within a few yards, and reined his horse to a stop directly in their path. If they were to continue, Jones and Van Vliet either would have to go around or through him, neither option seeming too smart at the moment.

The man did not speak, but his piercing, pale eyes seemed to bore straight through them.

"Them fires you two gents saw last night," Porter Rockwell said at length, nodding toward the canyon's rims, "warmed units of the Nauvoo Legion. Seems kind of hateful havin' t' spend yer nights in a place like this, 'specially with yer wife and family back in Salt Lake—huh?"

"Wasn't any bed of roses for us, either," Obediah said, gently sparring with this intense, long-haired stranger.

"Far as I know, ain't nobody makin' ya stay," Rockwell shot back. "Least bothersome way outta here is the way ya came. Smart thing t' do," he said, poking his long rifle in their direction, "is turn around and go back where ya came from—an' take all yer friends back there with ya."

"Well...y' see we...."

"I'm afraid we can't do that yet," Van Vliet broke in. "If we are all to end this...this...."

"Invasion," Rockwell spat at the two.

"Well...calling it what it is, yes...invasion."

"Well?"

"If I can meet with Brigham Young, then maybe—just maybe—we can bring this unfortunate situation to a peaceful end."

"That's where we're headed," Obediah said. "Captain

Van Vliet, here, hopes to get things turned around. He's been sent to talk with President Young."

Orrin Porter Rockwell's eyes focused sharply on Obediah Jones. Responding to this stranger's respectful use of his Prophet's name and title, he said, "An' just what d'you know about President Young?"

"Well, maybe I've been there before," Obediah said, his irritation with this stranger beginning to show. "I was...."

"If you been there before, ain't much need fer you t' go there again. Best I take the Captain where he needs t' go."

Obediah stiffened at the challenge, but the man's manner and the situation left little room for argument.

"Perhaps he's right, Mr. Jones," Van Vliet said, sensing the urgency to defuse the growing confrontation. "No need in both of us going."

"But if I...."

"Ain't nothin' going to happen t' this man," Porter Rockwell said, nodding toward Van Vliet. "He'll be in Salt Lake tomorrow, safe an' sound in President Young's parlor. Ain't nobody gonna do him harm when he's with me. Ain't nobody what'd hurt 'im anyways, prob'ly—not since he had the sense t' leave that pack of rabble behind."

Obediah Jones had not grown older all of these years because he was stupid. He knew when he was out-gunned and when further argument would quickly prove useless, if not downright dangerous.

"It appears you're right, Captain Van Vliet. It looks like this is the end of this trail for me. Our friend here seems to hold all the high cards."

"A right penetratin' observation," Porter Rockwell snickered, casually glancing up at the cliffs that towered above them. "My guess is there must be forty or so guns of one kind or other pointin' in our general direction 'bout now." His hand became lost in his long, thick beard as he scratched his chin. "Ma'be more'n that."

"Turn back, Mr. Jones," Van Vliet said, staring hard at Rockwell. "Somehow, I don't think there'll be trouble before I talk to Brigham Young."

"Least wise not if you and me get to Pres'dent Young b'fore your army gets t' here," Rockwell offered.

"Besides," the Captain continued, "Alexander will need your help if he is going to make much headway before I get back."

Porter Rockwell shoved his rifle into its place beneath his leg as he reined his horse around, and said, "Let's all be movin', then."

Obediah Jones resentfully watched the two men as they cantered off toward the towering granite wall that formed the western end of the canyon. Before they crossed a stream and disappeared into the willows and brush, the bearded man turned in his saddle and looked back at the army scout. It was a long, hard look, a stare that left little doubt as to who had the upper hand in this situation.

Glancing at the towering cliffs above him, Obediah reined his horse around, heaved a sigh, and moodily started the long trip back to Alexander's command, where he had little doubt that he would be needed. Benko Tatum might know his way around, but he was no scout.

Obediah smiled as he thought of one of Jasper Pughsey's conclusions where Tatum was concerned: "Couldn't find 'is way out of a small tepee," the mountain man had gleefully concluded one day, when he and Obediah had eluded Tatum and his gang after a particularly nasty run-in.

Obediah and Jasper had found one of their trapper friends laying outside the hut he had built back into a deep, dry cutbank where he lived with a Sioux squaw he had taken to wife.

The hut—little more than a cave with a front wall of logs and a short narrow door that hung on leather straps for hinges—was badly damaged, and the trapper lay bleeding and half conscious in the dirt, his frightened squaw struggling to help him. The man had been badly beaten, and judging from the difficulty he had breathing, suffered from some broken ribs.

It was not an unfamiliar story. The trapper had had a good season, and his hut was full of beaver, fox, and other furs. He was preparing to leave to meet with a trader when Benko Tatum and his men rode into his camp. It hadn't taken long, one man against seven or eight. His wife had run screaming into the forest, but the mountain man was clubbed nearly senseless by Tatum and his thugs who helped themselves to the rich cache of fur and left him for dead.

Doing what they could for their friend, Obediah and Jasper had taken after the gang, and before nightfall the next day they had found Tatum's camp several miles south of the trapper's hut.

Though it had been at least fifteen years, Obediah could remember what happened as if it were yesterday.

"Let's skin them coons and take their hides with the rest of the furs," Jasper said, surveying the careless camp site of the Tatum gang.

"Sometimes," Obediah observed piously, much to Jasper's annoyance, "it's better to teach a hard lesson than to administer a whipping."

"An' jest how do we do thet?"

"Through stealth and cunning," Obediah said. "A natural consequence of superior intelligence. Something which ought to be obvious even to you."

"Oh, yeah...well this jest might not...."

"Yeah...and this looks like as good a time as any. Why not let them wake up and find all that fur gone, along with some of their horses, and them never knowing what happened?"

"Hmm...does have kind of a nice ring t' it," Jasper said, rubbing his chin.

The gang had left one careless guard to raise any necessary alarm. But after not too gently putting him to sleep, the two mountain men had spent the night stealing all but one or two of the gang's horses, removing the furs from the sleeping men's camp, and hiding the plunder in a canyon about a mile and a half away.

By morning's first light, the two conspirators were back in their place behind a log hidden among the trees atop a small hill about fifty yards distant from the camp, both anxious to observe the gang's reaction to their stealth and cunning, as Obediah had put it.

As both knew he would, when Tatum saw that they had been robbed blind, he reacted with explosive violence, cussing and kicking the men within his reach, most of whom were still in their bedrolls. It was not long before the entire camp was engulfed in a loud, brawling fistfight.

"What did I tell ya?" Obediah said, with a laugh. "They'll never go back to Zeb's place."

"Now...what make's ya s'sure of thet?" Jasper asked, between chuckles.

"Because they think they left him dead...or so beat up

he couldn't move. And once they quit fightin' and find our trail south, they won't even think of going back in that direction."

Within a few minutes, three men lay unconscious on the ground still in their underwear, and the rest were beginning to concentrate on Benko Tatum for starting the ruckus.

Watching his old nemesis getting the worst of the fracas, Jasper Pughsey started to laugh, and he laughed so hard he couldn't help a loud snort as he struggled for breath.

To Obediah, ducking down behind the log that hid them, that snort sounded like it came from a hungry grizzly bear grunting and scratching for grubs. That snort was so loud that it seemed to echo against the nearby bluffs and through the surrounding pines, and Obediah thought the rude, reverberating sound would never die. But die it did, as the forest fell silent.

Jasper's laughter was uncontrolled, and it seemed to Obediah that his delighted partner had lost whatever concern he may have had for further safety. Raising his head to peer over the log at the now silent camp, Obediah froze. Just as he feared, with his partner's snort, the fighting had come to a sudden stop, and every man that remained on his feet was staring directly at Jasper Pughsey.

Jasper's laughter slowly trailed of into a sigh of despair as he realized what had happened, and both sides seemed frozen in disbelief.

"Get those dirty da...!"

Neither Obediah nor Jasper waited to hear the rest. They knew exactly what would come next, as they took off in a dead run for the canyon where their cleverly acquired booty was hidden.

Two of Tatum's men, in their haste to grab their pants

and guns, ran headlong into one another, each falling stunned to the ground.

Grabbing his Hawken, hoping for at least one good shot, Benko Tatum turned to chase after Obediah and Jasper, but in his anger and haste tripped over his two prostrate companions and fell head-first into the hot ashes and coals of the last night's fire.

As the surprised Tatum plowed into the dying remains of the fire, his prized Hawken flew from his grasp and slammed into the base of one of the nearby pines that surrounded the camp, breaking the stock immediately behind the breach, and discharging its load into the leg of one of the men struggling to get into his pants. Grabbing his shattered and bleeding leg, the man fell to the ground moaning in agony.

Maddened with frustration and pain, Tatum struggled up out of the ashes in a dusty, gray cloud, like some wild, wounded monster—half man, half beast—clawing at his clogged, painfully burning eyes.

Aside from the temporarily blinded Tatum, only one man remained on his feet in the ruined camp, and he stared in disbelief at the wreckage of broken bodies and camp supplies that lay cluttered around him.

Tatum managed to get one eye pried open, and yelled, "Well...go get 'em, you stupid...."

"I'll get 'em, boss," the man said, as he slowly backed away from the enraged Tatum. "I'll get 'em...don't you worry none."

"Get 'em...," Tatum hollered, rubbing his eyes and sinking to his knees.

The man turned and ran for the two remaining horses. Before Tatum knew what the outlaw was doing, he had untied the first animal he had come to and rode off in the opposite direction at a fast gallop, leaving his saddle and belongings behind.

Obediah's horse stumbled as it slid down a shallow scree in the canyon floor, snapping him back to the present. He couldn't help grinning at the thought of Jasper and how they had gotten those furs back to where they belonged. It was months before either of them discovered why Tatum and his men had not pursued them that wild, confusing morning.

They had been at a rendezvous some months later and the story had gotten around, maybe too much. Obediah knew that the last thing Benko Tatum could tolerate was being made the brunt of some tall tale. Among the mountain men, even the smallest story soon grew to buffalo-sized proportions.

Late one night, when Jasper had finished adding more detail to the latest version of the story, he had turned to Obediah and said, "It don't matter none, Obediah, thet coon couldn't find 'is way out of a small tepee."

"Yeah...and you and I know how true that is," Obediah had responded. "When he's riled, he's mean. We haven't heard the last of that, old beaver."

For some reason, the thought of Benko Tatum scouting the trail for Alexander and his men greatly disturbed the scout, and not just because of the animosity that lay between Tatum and him.

Watching Tatum and his cronies over the past weeks, Obediah had never been able to figure out why Benko Tatum, of all people, was scouting for the Utah expedition.

From the moment he had laid eyes on Tatum back at Fort Leavenworth, he had had the uncomfortable feeling that something was wrong; that Tatum was somehow out of place; that the man did not belong.

Why would he be helping the army march against the Mormons? he thought. *Where had he crossed trails with them before? Or did he have some purpose in getting out to the Utah Territory and scouting for the army because that was the easiest way of getting there? Or was it more likely that he was interested in seeing war? Seeing people hurt—or someone in particular hurt?*

Come t' think of it, Obediah thought, *how did Jasper Pughsey get into all of this? What was his role? Or was he in it at all? Why did he draw a bead on Benko Tatum? And why, when he had Tatum in his sights, didn't he do the world a favor and do the job right? What was he doing out on the prairie so far from the mountains in the first place?*

Before crossing a small stream that traversed the canyon, Obediah reined up and allowed his horse to drink.

"I'll tell ya," he mumbled to the horse, as he dismounted, "it's enough to give a man a headache."

Three days later Obediah Jones leaned over the horn of his saddle peering through the pines from atop a small knoll a hundred yards from the newly-finished rock walls of the Fort Bridger compound, and he didn't like what he saw. "Benko Tatum," he whispered to himself. "What's he doing here?"

Tatum and four mountain men were standing in front of the building that served as a trading post. They were in deep conversation as they loaded supplies on three packhorses. Six other horses stood at the hitching rail. From where he sat, Obediah could not hear what was being said, but he had no trouble identifying Tatum from the way the bald mountain man swung his arms in emphasis as he gave direction to the other four.

From where he sat, Obediah thought he recognized two of Tatum's companions from his encounter with them back at Fort Leavenworth, but the others were strangers. It was a troubling sight, because none of the men had been with Tatum when the army left Leavenworth.

Obediah cantered off the hill, and seeing no way to avoid being recognized, crossed the open meadow, and entered the compound through the heavy front gate. Tying his horse to the hitching rail in front of the nearest building, he quickly stepped between it and the trading post. Busy with their packing and scheming, neither Tatum or the others had noticed him, but it would be impossible to get any nearer without walking right past them.

There was no mistaking Tatum's raspy, conniving voice. "...and there's them in Kansas an' elsewhere what'd give a purty penny fer any guns 'r supplies we can fetch to 'em," he was saying.

"Yer talkin' foolhardy, Tatum," one of his companions responded. "That there's an army...we ain't jest gonna walk up and relieve them blue-bellies of their stuff. I say it cain't be done."

"Keep yer voice down," Tatum hissed. "I tell ya it can be done. Course we ain't gonna walk up an' take nothin'. What we got us here is a natural-borne war in the makin'. An' any man worth 'is salt can take advantage of it."

"Fer instance?" one asked.

"Yeah?" several joined in, rising to the bait.

"Ya got these Mormons out in the basin blackin' their dumb faces against this here army what's intent on makin' war with 'em, an' I tell ya it's gonna happen. I been with 'em. Alexander's gonna get his Tenth Infantry through these mountains come hell 'r high water, and we already know what the Mormon's 'r plannin' t' do. That coon Pughsey already busted us up purty good with a simple stampede in a rain storm, 'an on top a that, there's been a supply train 'r two burned."

"So how's that gonna get them army supplies inta our hands?" one of the men asked.

"Well now...jest suppose we help mix things up a bit, huh?"

"Yeah?"

"Pughsey's scoutin' fer the Mormons and Jones is scoutin' fer the army with me, an'...."

Obediah leaned against the rough logs of the building. *I knew Jasper was in this somehow*, he thought. *I've seen his sign all over the....*

The screened door of the trading post slammed as a tall, thin man, his arms filled with three Hawken rifles, black powder, and galena, joined the others. "We've got enough powder and ball t' kill every livin' thing between here and Great Salt Lake," he said. It was Will Teeter. Obediah Jones would have known his voice anywhere.

Laughter was coming from the group as Tatum said, "Yeah...an' with that dumb coon Pughsey soon dead, we're gonna stir up all kinds a trouble ourselves. All it's gonna take t' get the party started is a few shots at the Mormons an' a few shots at the army. Then we jest sit back an' take advantage of the confusion. We can look like Mormons, and burn a few army supply trains as well as that dumb Pughsey an' his bunch can."

"Yeah," one of the men said, "an' with Pughsey outta the way, ya can lay the blame on him."

"I'm glad somebody's finally catchin' on," Tatum said,

with disgust.

"That's right. We do some burnin' and takin'," Teeter said, "and lay the blame on Pughsey and the Mormons."

The voices became confused as all joined in murmurs of agreement, and Obediah strained to catch more detail.

"'at's it...an' knock off a few Mormons an' they'll start shootin' in every direction," Tatum concluded.

"When do we start?" Teeter asked.

"Ain't no point in waitin'," Tatum said. "Pughsey ain't goin' nowheres...permanent-like soon as we get these supplies back up there tomorrow. Jones is visitin' the Mormons with that Captain Van Vliet. I tell ya, ain't no way it could be better. Everybody's hopin' fer peace, but I'll garntee ya there ain't gonna be none."

"So...what's in it fer you," one of the men asked, "and what's in it fer us?"

"Money fer all of us, Jones an' Pughsey fer me. I been waitin' a long time fer this. I'm gonna take care a Pughsey b'fore we leave camp tomorrow—an' Jones when the shootin' starts."

"An' what about Teeter...what's he got in this?"

Obediah strained to hear more, but Teeter's answer was lost as the men mounted the porch and entered the trading post. Not wanting to believe what he heard, the scout quickly made his way back to his horse. First he had to find where Tatum had Jasper Pughsey penned up and save his skin, and then the two of them would find a way to upset Tatum's plans.

The potential for a winter of prolonged war, a war nobody could win, was dangerously high. It had to be stopped.

* * *

The wide, neatly laid-out streets of Great Salt Lake City had been a welcome sight after weeks on the trail, though the heat of the valley was somewhat surprising to Van Vliet after the chill of the mountains. From the moment he arrived, he had been made welcome and treated with the respect due a Chief of State. Sipping a cold glass of fresh lemonade on this quiet Sabbath morning, the soldier sat stiffly in the front parlor of Brigham Young's comfortably furnished home listening to the hushed activity of its occupants as they prepared for the unusual excitement of the coming day.

Staring through the lace curtains covering the window, he could see a steady stream of people—Saints, Brigham Young always called them—passing the Young compound toward their meeting place further down the street. From all he could tell, they were an industrious, peaceful people intent on worshiping God in their own way. *None of this makes sense*, he thought. *Why on earth are we....*

"Good morning, Captain Van Vliet," Brigham Young said, quietly closing the parlor door behind him.

"Good morning, sir," Van Vliet said, jumping to his feet.

"I trust you've had a good night's rest?"

"Well...yes...I...."

"It's time we left for the meeting, Captain. It will be a long one, and we don't want to be the cause of its lateness."

"No sir. In fact, I'm anxious to return to my command and report on what we've discussed," Van Vliet said, as the two men left the house and stepped into the Mormon leader's carriage.

"Our meeting will be held in the bowery, Captain. We are as desirous as you to bring this invasion to an end and forestall the violence that will surely result if our efforts fail. I expect the crowd will be a large one. As you can imagine, the people here are anxious about their future."

"I can certainly understand that, sir."

The unusually wide street was crowded with people on foot, on horseback, and in buggies, a tidy river of humanity flowing with purpose. The Mormon Prophet's carriage, with its two, intent occupants, melted with the crowd and soon drew up behind the Bowery.

"I'd say most of them feel that they have been driven about a league too far once too often—at least that's how I'm feeling, Captain," Brigham Young said, as the two stepped from the carriage.

Entering a spacious, open shelter—the bowery, President Young had called it—Van Vliet followed the Mormon leader up on to a broad, wooden platform that ran the entire width of the bowery and contained a number of chairs and a solidly built podium. After shaking what seemed to Van Vliet countless hands and nodding to large numbers of smiling faces, the two men took their seats on the front row facing the audience.

Van Vliet was struck by the novelty of the place. Hundreds—probably thousands—of people were settling with anticipation into their places under a roof of thatched pine and other bows supported by what seemed like a forest of large, widely spaced posts. For the most part, the sides of the bowery were open, and a cool breeze provided a welcome comfort to the assembly.

The meeting began with a song, and the large crowd sang with a unity that struck Van Vliet as almost choir-like in quality, but the beauty of the music was followed with a prayer that quickly brought forward the underlying purpose of the meeting. The morning soon began to seem endless, and the constant references of the speakers to the invading army made Van Vliet uncomfortable sitting in full view of the huge crowd. The soldier fought to stifle a sigh of relief as he began to sense that the meeting was coming to an end, when abruptly Brigham Young rose to his feet and stepped to the podium. *Here it comes,* he thought—*the final word.*

"Before the meeting closes, I want to make a few remarks," the Prophet said, as he gripped the podium and looked out into the faces of the people for whom he knew the Lord would hold him responsible. "My feelings are so complicated that I want to say a few words, yet I don't want to say anything. Suffice it to say that I am angry. I feel a righteous anger, and furthermore the bosom of the Almighty burns with anger toward those scoundrels whose intentions are to do us harm."

A stir of agreement and shared anger ran through the crowd as their leader warmed to the indignation and irritation that he so obviously felt. Van Vliet shifted uncomfortably in his seat, feeling a thousand eyes boring into his soul. Despite the fact that he had been treated with the utmost respect—even friendliness—he knew that to these people, he represented the enemy, an enemy sworn to destroy their way of life.

"...and hellish abuse," the Prophet continued, "and we will not bear any more of it; for there is no just law requiring further forbearance on our part."

Van Vliet knew it was true. *There was no point to what was being done,* he thought. *There was no need for an army here; these were a peaceful, friendly people, and they did not deserve what was happening. He had to get back and put a stop to it. He had to get to....*

"...Van Vliet, who is now on the stand, to come here and learn whether he could procure the necessary supplies for the army."

What gall, Van Vliet thought, *for me to be here asking this people to provide supplies for the army that is to invade them. What justice is there....*

"...of you have been previously acquainted with the Captain. Captain Van Vliet visited us in Winter Quarters; and, if I remember correctly, he was then officiating as Assistant Quartermaster. He is again in our midst in the capacity of Assistant Quartermaster. From the day of his visit to Winter Quarters, many of this people have become personally acquainted with him. I have always found him to be free and frank, and to be a man that wishes to do right; and no doubt he would deal out justice to all, if he had the power."

Van Vliet began to relax, feeling the influence of the Mormon leader's generous remarks. *Yes,* the soldier thought, *this can be worked out. There can be....*

"...cause of this hostile feeling against this people? Brother Taylor has been telling you. God has restored the Gospel of salvation to earth again. That unites the hearts of the people, brings together those of different nations, notwithstanding their various traditions and their different manners and customs, and makes them of one heart and of one mind. And what follows? All hell is moved against them, because the kingdoms of this world—the kingdoms of darkness—are in danger. All hell is moved against this people, because we are of one heart and of one mind."

Van Vliet's mind was filled with the anomalies, the impossibilities of the situation. He was the representative of a government, the power of which rested on the

Constitution of the United States. It was a Constitution that provided the utmost freedom for its citizens, investing full sovereign authority in them by limiting the powers of those whom they elected to govern them—serve would be a better word. Yet, those very leaders, that government, under that same constitution, had sent an expeditionary army here to oppress them. And that's what it was, oppression. He could see no evidence of rebellion, he had heard no words of treason, he had no business being here, and he knew it.

"So where are we?" the Prophet asked, his voice calm. "Here is where we are: there is a wicked anger, and there is a righteous anger. The Lord does not suffer wicked anger to be in his heart; but there is anger in his bosom, and he will hold a controversy with the nations, and will sift them, and no power can stay his hand."

Glancing briefly at Van Vliet, the Mormon leader continued, "The government of our country will go by the board through its own corruptions, and no power can save it. If we can avert the blow for another season, it is probable that our enemies will have enough to attend to at home, without worrying about the Latter-day Saints."

The worrisome thing is, Van Vliet thought, *with Kansas turmoil and talk of secession in the South, the man may be right—can't help but wonder what he knows that the rest of us don't. The government I represent, while it is determined to defeat the Mormons, is itself on the brink of disaster. The whole thing is likely to go up in flames from its own internal friction, and our leaders send an army out here to accomplish who knows what.*

"That being the case, I am perfectly willing that the brethren should stop all improvements, if they choose, and spend a few years in seeing what our enemies will do;

though their efforts against us will only tend to use them up the faster."

Van Vliet sat straighter in his chair. *Here comes my answer*, he thought. *This is the final word.*

"Suppose that our enemies send 50,000 troops here, they will have to transport all that will be requisite to sustain them over one winter; for I will promise them, before they come," the Prophet said, thumping the pulpit for emphasis, each word falling like a hammer-blow, "that there shall not be one particle of forage, nor one mouthful of food for them, should they come."

Brigham Young looked directly at Captain Van Vliet, and said, "They will have to bring all their provisions and forage." Turning back to the assembly, he continued, "And though they start their teams with as heavy loads as they can draw, there is no team that can bring enough to sustain itself, to say nothing of the men.

"It strikes me, Brothers and Sisters, that it would be far cheaper for the Government to pay the debts they honestly owe us, and leave us unmolested in the peaceful enjoyment of our rights."

Brigham Young's refusal amounted to little more than Van Vliet had expected, though he certainly did not anticipate that the message would be delivered with such force and in such an embarrassingly public way. *But, after all*, he thought, *what kind of reaction could one expect from a leader that was being asked to provision the army that was intent on destroying him?*

"...man or woman who is not willing to destroy anything and everything of their property that would be of use to the enemy..."

A thoroughly experienced soldier, Van Vliet had

expected all that he had heard so far, but he was totally unprepared for the words that now broke rudely into his thoughts.

"...and I again say so today; for when the time comes to burn and lay waste our improvements, if any man undertakes to shield his, he will be sheared down; for 'judgment will be laid to the line and righteousness to the plummet.' Now the faint-hearted can go in peace; but should that time come they must not interfere," the Mormon Prophet said, thumping the podium with his forefinger.

The Prophet stood silent as his words settled among the assembled Saints. The only sound Van Vliet could hear in the bowery was the soothing sound of the gentle wind in the bows over his head, the only reaction in the determined faces before him, a united resolve to stand firm.

"Before I will suffer what I have in times gone by, there shall not be one building, nor one foot of lumber, nor a stick, nor a tree, nor a particle of grass and hay, that will burn, left in reach of our enemies."

Captain Van Vliet looked into the face of a Prophet whose words came like angry balls of lead: "I am sworn, if driven to extremity, to utterly lay waste, in the name of Israel's God."

And Van Vliet knew it was true.

CHAPTER EIGHT

Leaving Fort Bridger, Obediah urged his horse through the surrounding meadow, splashed across a stream, and rode into a small stand of trees where he had an excellent view of the fort's sturdy south gate. The air was clean and crisp, and there was a cold breeze blowing off the mountains to the west that kept the trees around him in constant agitation. The dappled shade from the disquieted leaves offered excellent concealment, as an impatient Obediah Jones waited for Tatum and his gang to head back to their hideout.

The sun was low in the western sky when the Tatum gang emerged from the fort, rode around its southeast corner, and headed north toward the mountains. Spurring their mounts forward, they rode as briskly as possible with three heavily laden pack horses, obviously trying to make good time while the daylight lasted.

Hanging back as far as he could without losing sight of the riders through the brush and trees, Obediah tried to make himself as invisible as possible, keeping off the trail and staying well within the tree line. It was hard going, and because Tatum and his men were using a dim but familiar trail, Obediah had a hard time keeping them in sight.

As darkness closed in, the six disappeared into the blackness of a deep, heavily wooded ravine that split the mountain they had been skirting and emptied out onto a wide valley several miles to the east. Obediah dismounted and cautiously approached the spot where the dim trail disappeared over the edge. Though heavily timbered, both sides of the ravine were rimmed with massive outcroppings of solid rock.

From where Obediah stood, the trail dropped steeply through a large crack in the rimrock and became lost as it twisted toward the bottom through a maze of trees and large boulders, barely visible in the darkness below. The mountain man knew that if Tatum or one of his men had caught sight of him, this would be a likely place to get bushwhacked. Fairly certain that his presence had not been discovered, Obediah remounted and urged his horse over the edge and down through the disorder and confusion of the dark, rocky ravine.

As night had fallen, the wind had freshened and grown more persistent, and the constant motion of the trees obscured any other movement or sound. But there was no sign of the gang as Obediah reached the bottom and a fork in the trail, one leading up into the night, and the other apparently leading down off the mountain and out into the open valley. Both trails quickly become lost in the broken gravel and stony rubble of the dry river bed that served as the floor of the deep ravine.

Dismounting, Obediah knelt down and studied the jumble of river stone and sand. There was no trail here, just the confusion of fallen trees, branches, and brush left by the last flash flood to come roaring off the mountain, taking everything in its path and obliterating any trail that may have started to appear since the last such storm.

There were few trackers in the mountains better than Obediah Jones—unless it was Jasper Pughsey, and even that was arguable. Studying each stone, worn smooth by centuries of abrasive floods, the scout found a white gash scraped into one, and then another and another further along. The riders had gone upstream, the iron shoes of their horses chipping and turning the rocks as they struggled through the debris of the river bed.

Struggling up the narrowing ravine, Obediah found the point at which the six riders had climbed out of the streambed, following a slim trail that led up the side of the precipitous cutbank and into the pines. A less practiced eye would have missed the trail altogether in the darkness.

Worried about what Benko Tatum would do when he reached his hideout, Obediah urged his horse at as fast a pace as the conditions of the trail would allow. They were high up now, and as the air thinned, the climb became more difficult for both man and horse. If Tatum had discovered he was being followed, there would have been a showdown before now.

The trail turned sharply downhill and curved to the left around a large outcropping of boulders. Obediah reined up at the edge of a small meadow and studied the layout of Benko Tatum's hideout. Eight horses stood in front of a small, dimly lit cabin. The other two structures were dark.

With as much caution as possible, Obediah led his horse through the pine and Quaking Aspen that surrounded the meadow in an effort to get to the back of the buildings, but a shaft of light stopped him as the cabin door suddenly opened.

"Did you hear somethin'?" one of the gang said, peering into the darkness. It was Will Teeter.

"A deer or somethin'," someone answered from inside. "These woods is full of 'em."

"Yeah...maybe," Teeter said, leaving the doorway and walking to the edge of the narrow wooden porch. "I still ain't s' sure we...."

"Start unpackin' them horses," Benko Tatum said, pushing his way past the man. "I'm gonna check on Pughsey."

Hearing Tatum's voice, Obediah froze and cupped his hand over his horse's nose. The wrong sound or movement now would really upset the apple cart. He could probably get away in the darkness, but it would certainly prove fatal for Jasper. No point in rushing things, he thought, holding the horse's head close to his.

The bald mountain man walked to the end cabin not far from where Obediah stood and peered into the darkness through a small, barred window set in the door.

"Leave 'im be," one of the men hollered, "'an help us get these supplies unloaded. T'morrow's time enough fer that coon."

Obediah relaxed as Tatum turned and joined the others in unpacking and unsaddling the horses. Taking advantage of the noise the men were making, Obediah led his horse deeper into the trees and tied the animal in a thick stand of Quaking Aspen and underbrush. Knowing now where Jasper was being held, he could relax and wait for the gang to settle down for the night.

"Psst...Jasper."

Jasper's eyes flipped open, and he tried to focus in the darkness of the cramped cell. "What the...where?" He was not quite awake, but he knew he had heard something.

"Psst...Pughsey...you in there?" a familiar voice whispered, more loudly this time.

"Well, I'll be...I don't believe wha...."

"Jasper, wake up before the rest of the world does," the

voice called, more urgently.

"Obediah Jones! Issat you?" Jasper hollered, springing from the cot. "Where are ya?"

"Of course it's me, and quiet down. I'm out here. Where'd you think?"

"Well...how'd ya...?"

"Oh, I heard you got your tail caught in a crack again and wound up in somebody's hoosegow. Even worse, I heard you'd gone under."

"Well, I never went under, an' my tail ain't in no crack, neither," Jasper shot back in exasperation. "I'm jest momentarily outta action is all."

"More's the pity, too," Obediah said. "Looks like a pretty determined place. I thought you were beyond all of this—a free spirit, so to speak."

"I'll tell ya what I am, I'm all penned up by thet snake Benko Tatum, an' all yer palaverin' ain't gettin' me outta here, thet's what. Now, stop yer talkin' an' do somethin'. Tatum's about t' slit my gizzard, an' if he don't, thet O'Riley feller's downright determined t' hang me."

"Sounds good to me."

"Hangin' me?"

"No...getting you out. What exactly do you suggest I do?"

"Well, now...ain't you the smart one," Jasper said, his temper rising. "Why don't you jest go an...." Jasper's voice trailed off as he peered around his dark cell.

"Yeah?"

"Well...lemme think. This place does appear t' be kinda substantial-like."

"Uh-huh. Looks like Tatum's got ya, alright.

"Yeah...well...ain't no wooden walls been built that can

hold this child fer long, yew can bet last winter's plews on thet. Wagh!"

"Uh-huh," Obediah said, his voice trailing away in the darkness as he ran his hand along the back wall of the jail. "Then...how come you're still in there?"

"Obediah? Where'd ya go? Get back over here, I...."

"Keep your shirt on, I'm right here," Obediah whispered, returning to the window. "And keep your voice low, we've jerked Tatum's tail too many times to take anymore chances than we need to."

"'At's true enough," Jasper chuckled, lowering his voice.

"This wall appears to be made of nothing but mud and straw bricks and some pine between the support beams."

"This side, too."

"Anyone else in there?"

"Nope, its jest me an' a few spiders. Appears the United States Army don't spend much time corrallin' each other up like maybe they oughta."

"Well, there are plenty who'd like to see more of you and your friends on your side of those bars, and when that army gets to Great Salt Lake City, things are likely to get crowded in hoosegows all over the territory. So, now's maybe the time for you to leave, because Tatum isn't going t' save your worthless hide for O'Riley—that you can count on."

"Now...jest what does all a thet mean? How come you're s' all fired knowin' about...."

"You know exactly what I mean. Nothing is going to stop this army, and they've got good reason, too. They've got orders, and those polygamists don't stand a chance."

"Obediah Jones...jest exactly what've...?"

"Don't go away, I'll be back," Obediah said, moving swiftly to the corner of the building.

"Go away?" Jasper, hollered through the bars. " Obediah, you come back here an...."

"Oh, hesh up," Obediah hissed, "I'll be back."

The old mountain man turned to face the dark room and laid back on his wood cot, surprised and troubled by Obediah's sudden appearance and the fact that he seemed to know more than Jasper would have guessed. He had not seen Obediah in years. Certainly, he hadn't been anywhere around this part of the territory.

When the beaver trade had all but disappeared, the two of them had begun to drift apart. Not long after arriving in the Salt Lake valley, Obediah had headed east, and Jasper strayed around the mountain country, always returning to the growing Mormon communities along the Wasatch. *Where had Obediah come from so suddenly?* Jasper thought. *What had he been doing all of this time? How had Obediah known about the army? He even seemed to know of its mission and the animosity its soldiers held for the Mormon people. And how did he know Tatum had him? And how did Obediah know where to find him?*

Yet, as Jasper had scouted the army wagon trains, something about their disposition—the way some of them used the trail and camped—had troubled him, something familiar in their tracks and dead camps. He could never quite put his finger on it, and that was unsettling to Jasper Pughsey.

One of the best trackers in the west, he had learned early to trust his instincts, and he disliked not being able to lay things to rest as he studied them. Tracks and camp sites are signatures, and he had seen a familiar hand in a number of them. Now, in the darkness of this cell, he suddenly knew it was the hand of his old friend, Obediah Jones.

A horse blew and stomped outside the window, and the end of a rope fell to the floor beneath the barred window.

"Tie that rope good and tight around three of those bars, and let's see what happens," Obediah said.

"Whatcha got in mind?" Jasper asked, tying the rope securely.

"If that wall is nothing but mud and logs, maybe I can pull those bars loose enough for you to crawl between them before somebody hears us, but we've got to hurry. It's going to start getting light pretty soon."

"Good idea...thet rope should hold now. Give 'er a yank," Jasper chuckled.

Tying his end of the rope to the saddle horn, Obediah dug his heels into the horse's flanks. The rope tightened on the bars and the prickly hairs on the rough hemp began to stand erect as it stretched with the strain. Obediah's horse leaned into the obstinate, unyielding shackle, and with repeated insistence from his master's rude heels the big gelding began to lunge against its cruel confinement, his hoofs scraping and kicking in the hard, dry earth. Dust began to fill the air, and something cracked. It was a loud crack, and the horse stumbled forward and shied, nearly throwing his rider, as the wall suddenly complained under the strain and bulged outward.

"Hold it, Obediah," Jasper hissed loudly, in an effort to be heard by no one but his buckskin-clad emancipator, who was struggling to stay mounted as he fought with his skittish horse. "Yer gonna have them coons down on us if ya keep this up."

"Me?...you're the one doing all the hollering," Obediah shot back, as he dismounted by the dusty, bloated wall. "Are the bars loose?"

"Naw...they're set tight in this here log frame," Jasper responded, pushing at the stubborn bars. "I wonder how they got 'em in there in the first place," he said, studying the solid window casement more closely. "Yer gonna hafta pull the whole thing free if I'm ever gonna get outta this place."

"Well," Obediah said, mounting his nervous horse, "I'm not convinced you're worth all this trouble, anyway."

Something thumped the ceiling above Jasper's head. "What in tarnation's goin' on down there?" a sleep-drugged voice croaked.

"Why didn't ya tell me someone was up there?" Obediah hissed, as more movement could be heard in the room above.

"'Cause I didn't know they was?"

"You didn't know they...?"

"If you don't hurry, the whole bunch of 'em's gonna show up, an' old Benko Tatum'd just love to put you in here with me. Purty picture, huh?" Jasper said, above the increasing noise of shuffling feet and thumping boots from the room above.

"Well...another good tug on this rope and you should be outta there."

With more urging, Obediah's reluctant horse leaned into the rope, and the barred window casement broke free from the bulging, weakened wall. The heavy solid casing did not break apart, but tumbled loudly to the ground in a shower of dust, bringing large chunks of the surrounding wall with it.

"Somebody go get Benko," a voice hollered from above, "an' hurry up about it!" A door slammed and someone thumped down the outside stairs.

The sudden give of the casing caused the straining horse to stumble forward, but regaining its balance, the frightened animal bolted and kicked wildly at the noise and confusion behind it, unseating its rider who landed painfully and unceremoniously in the dirt. Freed from the stubborn wall, the frightened horse galloped off into the darkness, the heavy window casement tumbling behind it, crashing through the trees and underbrush. Obediah rolled over and looked up to see the dark form of the cabin wall begin to slowly twist with a loud groan and sink toward him. The air was filled with the wrenching sound of splintering wood and braces as joints separated and the wall collapsed outward.

With the sudden loss of support, the top floor and roof of the cabin suddenly sagged, slowly sank and then crashed into what remained of the bottom half of the structure.

Howling and cursing, the men caught in the room above fell through the separating floor into the devastation below as the entire cabin tumbled into utter ruin.

"Let's get," Jasper Pughsey offered, as he ran out of the dust past his prostrate friend. "This ain't no time t' be relaxin'."

A gentle breeze played at the sides of the tent causing the shadows cast by the lamps to dance merrily around the men as they enjoyed their evening meal. Lieutenant General Daniel H. Wells helped himself to another large serving of creamed peas and potatoes, took a bite, and leaned back in his chair, contemplating the young officer seated across the small but crowded table.

"Not bad for soldier's food, hmm?" the General said,

enjoying this time with his officers.

Major Lot Smith looked up from his plate, "Yes, sir. I suppose even the worst of times can bring some enjoyment."

"Not a bad observation, Major. These surely are not the best of times, but we are going to turn them to our advantage...hopefully sooner than later," said the General, smiling at the assembled members of his staff. "If you're smart...and I have little doubt of that...you'll continue to have your moments of comfort—only at the expense of your unreasonable Uncle Sam. Judging from all we hear, his wagon trains are plentifully laden."

Glancing at the other officers, Lot Smith set his fork beside his empty plate and studied the face of the Mormon General. "Yes, sir. And how would you like me to proceed to do that?"

"Major Smith, we are short on everything but brains, experience, and dedication. The Army of the United States would appear to be flush with every needful commodity, but sadly lacking in those rare qualities. Therein lies our strength and the invading army's weakness."

"Yes, sir."

"Gentlemen," the General said, addressing the assembled group, "thanks to Major Smith, here, and Porter Rockwell, we now know with some certainty the size and disposition of the leading elements of the invading force, and we can guess...quite accurately, I think...what their intentions are."

A junior officer at the far end of the table leaned forward and said, "Sir...some of us have heard little more than rumors. How big is that force?"

"We have known for some time, Lieutenant Abbott, that

we can expect the army to eventually have some 2,500 troopers in its ranks. But Port Rockwell has just informed us that, as of now, there would appear to be approximately 1,200 soldiers on the march."

"Rockwell has returned?" someone asked from the other end of the table.

"Yes...he has," Smith responded. "I sent him and Jasper Pughsey out on a scouting expedition several weeks ago. They not only found what we suppose to be the leading elements of the army, they were able to track it and study it closely."

"Not only that gentlemen," the General said, tapping his glass in an effort to quiet the men at the table. "...they have seen to it that the enemy felt our sting—nothing too terribly painful, but our sting nonetheless. As some of you know, one of our advance units managed to sneak in and burn a few supply wagons, but Porter Rockwell tells me that, in addition, one of their large bivouacs was recently broken up by an unexpected stampede of their own cattle."

The tent buzzed with appreciative laughter and chatter as the assembled officers reacted to the news that the invading army was beginning to experience a little of what lay in store for them.

"Sir...is there any...?"

"Gentlemen...please," the General said, rapping his glass for attention. "One at a time...please. I'm sorry...Colonel Cummings?"

"Is there any hope, sir, that Van Vliet will be able to dissuade his superiors, or the politicians behind this infernal mischief, before things have gotten beyond recall?"

"We can only hope so, Colonel Cummings," General Wells said, pushing back his chair and rising. "But our biggest mistake would be to rest on such a hope. That is, simply put, a luxury we cannot afford. Besides, President Young issued our proclamation over a week ago forbidding the army to enter Utah, and he did that after rather extensive talks with Van Vliet, as you all know. I think the time has now...ah, Gentlemen, to top things off, here comes the pie."

Four troopers, arms burdened with large, golden-crusted apple pies, were greeted with enthusiastic applause by the eager men at the table. The tent quickly filled with the tart, spicy smell of the bulky pies, their sweet fillings bursting from beneath their flaky crusts as each was cut.

With each man turning to the tasty, solitary task before him, the chill of the evening air became heavy with the most tantalizing aroma of autumn, and the realities facing each were momentarily forgotten.

Finally, waving off a trooper with a third piece of pie, General Wells gave a great sigh and pushed his plate away. "May the peace and enjoyment of this fine meal return to these mountains quickly...and for all."

His words were greeted with a chorus of "amen" from around the comfortably cluttered table.

"I would like to end this meeting on this pleasant note, but the demands of our situation require one or two additional tasks." Turning to Lot Smith, he continued, "Lot, you are hereby appointed Major of the First Battalion of Cavalry."

Taken somewhat by surprise, Lot Smith responded, "Well, thank you...sir...I...."

"Don't be too anxious to thank me, Major. Yours will be a fairly heavy burden, as it has been in the past."

"Yes, sir."

"Could you take a few good men and turn some of those wagons back that are presently on the road..."

Lot Smith leaned forward, a grin splitting his face, "Yes, sir," he said with undue emphasis.

"...or burn them?"

"Now, that I can do—with a few good men and a great deal of pleasure."

"Major," the General said, pushing his chair back from the table, "You are free to form your First Battalion, as humble as it is going to be. I can give you Captain Haight and Lieutenants Abbott and Vance. You may select the others.

"As I said before, Major, by taking advantage of what our invaders lack, we can deny them what they seem to have in abundance, and in the future, you may feast upon their supplies."

"I would like to hand pick my men," Smith said, breaking into the appreciative laughter of the others.

"Done...but no more than forty."

"Forty it is, sir—if I can have Jasper Pughsey as scout."

"Why Pughsey? Why not Porter Rockwell or Hickman or one of the others?"

Colonel Albert P. Rockwell, head of field operations, leaned forward and said, "If I'm not mistaken, sir, both have left to scout the progress of the advanced wagon trains you spoke of, General Wells."

"As you know, sir, I sent Pughsey out with Rockwell several weeks ago, and Rockwell says he's one of the finest scouts he's ever met. But, I'd take 'im anyway, sir," Smith said, reflectively. "There's something about the man...I don't know exactly. He's been in the mountains for at least thirty years, and...he's...solid. Besides, he knows the lay of the land from here to the Mississippi."

"Are you sure he can be trusted?"

"I've only spoken with 'im once, General. I can't say that I know him, but I sense that I know him, if you get my drift, sir. Rockwell says that, inside, Pughsey's one of us. I don't know why, but...yes...he can be trusted."

One of the others at the table spoke up. "Rockwell certainly trusts 'im."

Several others joined in agreement.

"Well...I have no reason not to, I suppose," General Wells said, pushing himself away from the table and leaning back in his chair. "It's just that...well...frankly, he's not really one of us."

"I think he is in spirit, sir," Smith responded, leaning across the table toward the General. "I not only trust him, I feel like I need 'im."

"Then I shall reserve judgement. When can I meet him, Major?"

"Well, sir, I can't rightly say."

"You can't rightly say?"

"No sir," Lot Smith said, clearing his throat. "It would appear that the Army captured him when he stampeded their cattle through that bivouac Port Rockwell told you about."

"That was Pughsey's work?"

"Yes sir. He's caused them a good deal of discomfort on our behalf."

"Well...assuming you can get him back," the General said, with a chortle, "go ahead and use him, Major."

"Thank you, General Wells...we'll get him back—if he doesn't escape first," Smith said with relief.

"In the meantime, gentlemen, I will be leaving with

Colonels Jones and McAllister, here, for Echo Canyon, where they and their men will construct whatever fortifications are necessary at the narrows. In fact, they will be expected to construct whatever emplacements are necessary on the heights along the entire length of the canyon if necessary."

"We intend to have emplacements along both sides of the canyon," McAllister said, "to accommodate as many men as possible."

"When will you be leaving, sir?" one of the other officers asked.

"Probably Sunday next," the General said, looking at Jones and McAllister. "Will things be ready then, gentlemen?"

"They will, sir," Jones responded.

"While we don't want war, it is necessary to act with dispatch. That army will not pass through the narrows without President Young's permission, if it takes every man jack of us," Wells said.

The men pushed their chairs away from the table as General Wells stood up and walked to the tent flap and turned, and said, "If we are determined, we shall succeed—with the Lord's help."

"Sir," Lot Smith said, before the General could leave the officer's mess, "where will you be when things get started?"

Daniel Wells took a deep breath and looked at the floor, as if seeking an answer, and said, "I'm going to take a few men and go on to Fort Bridger. For the time being...that will be my forward command post."

"The Lord be with you, brethren. And thank you for a most enjoyable meal," the General said, as he ducked through the tent door and disappeared into the night.

* * *

The light of early morning was beginning to give shape to the pine-covered mountainside as Jasper Pughsey and Obediah Jones ran blindly through the dense forest, away from Benko Tatum's hide out. Thick brush covered the ground and caught at their feet, frustrating their progress, and their sweaty faces stung from the slap and bite of pine branches, making their escape more difficult.

"Hang on, Obediah," Jasper said, as he stopped and doubled over with his hands on his knees, his breath coming in hard gasps. "I gotta...get m' breath."

Gasping for air, Obediah leaned heavily against a tree and slowly slumped to the ground, the rough pine bark scratching through his cotton shirt. "This...isn't good, Jasper. Tatum isn't going t' let this...happen," he heaved. "That coon'll be madder than a hornet. Especially...since he's got plans we can louse up for him."

"We gotta get...that horse a yours. Did ya see where the fool thing went?"

"He took off across the meadow...probably back the way we came...to Fort Bridger. I don't know...things were happening...too fast."

His breath finally coming easier, Jasper stood up and walked back a few paces toward the hideout. "Now, jest what plans 're you talking about?"

"Hear anything?"

"Lotta ruckus 'n' hollerin'. They got horses, Obediah. Ain't gonna be long before...."

"Jasper...what if we outfoxed 'em."

"Well, it ain't been all thet hard in the past, I reckon. Whataya thinkin'?"

"We left a trail a blind man could follow."

"Well, what else could...?"

"Let's back-track toward the camp. Tatum won't expect us to hang around there," Obediah said, getting up and joining Jasper. "As soon as they've headed out on our trail, we can grab some supplies and light a shuck back to the Fort."

"Why back t' the fort?"

"We've got to warn them, and then I've got to get back to Alexander and warn him."

"Warn 'em about what?"

"Tatum's going to start this war on his own."

"Wha...?"

"He's determined to get both sides shooting. Then he's going to rob the supply trains and sell the goods t' the sectionalists and those talking war in the Kansas Territory and back in the states."

Benko Tatum stood looking at the ruined cabin as the dust slowly settled to the ground.

"You dumb coons," he growled. "We're gonna get those two, if it's the last thing we do." Slowly turning, he looked at his half-dressed gang. "You hear me?" he hollered, his voice echoing through the pines.

"Benko...we was...."

Tatum slowly pulled his knife from the scabbard at his side. "Which one a you dumb beavers was supposed t' be on guard?"

One of the men stepped back, and said, "Benko, nobody ever figgered he...."

"Ever figgered?" Benko mocked. "Sorta seems like nobody ever learned you t' figger straight," he said, jerking his stubby thumb toward the collapsed building, his voice rising. "Who're you t' be figgerin', anyways!? I do the figgerin' around here! You un'er stand me!?" he hollered.

"Ain't no point in this," Will Teeter offered, stepping forward. "While we're arguin' over spilt milk, them two coons'll be gettin' away."

"If they get away, somebody gets it in the lights," Tatum said, turning on the man, "and get this straight, Teeter, you might have it real urgent t' get back at them Mormons, but I'm the boss around here, and what I say goes."

"I got no argument with that, Tatum," Teeter said. "I ain't been here with ya long, and I ain't s' interested in whatever yer gonna steal, but...."

"Well...just what is it you do want?" Tatum sneered.

"You know what I want, Tatum. I want t' see Mormon blood fertilizin' these mountains. That's what I want," he said, squinting hard at Tatum. "They dealt me dirt and threw me out jest 'cause I was tradin' with them stinking redskins and makin' some money that didn't go t' old Brigham."

Tatum grinned. "That old he-coon ran ya off, huh?"

"I lost everything, and I aim t' get it back—one way or the other."

Turning toward the cabins, Tatum said, "Get the horses. We're goin' t' Fort Bridger."

"Fort Bridger?" one of the men asked. "What 're we gonna do there?"

"You three get the horses, like I tol' ya," Tatum said. Motioning to the others he walked toward the nearest cabin. As Tatum walked away, Teeter said, "Well now, if you was them two coons, knowin' what they seem t' know, where would you head?"

CHAPTER NINE

Jasper Pughsey and Obediah Jones lay concealed in deep grass beneath a thick stand of Quaking Aspen. The earth smelled damp in the late morning shade and the drying grasses of autumn rustled about them in the light breeze.

"One horse ain't gonna do it fer us, Obediah," Jasper said. "We're jest plain lucky we found thet spooky nag a yours."

"Well...we're not going to get one down there," Obediah responded, nodding toward the Fort that lay a good two hundred yards away. "Those fellas seem pretty intent on our seeing them and not getting too close."

Fort Bridger squatted on what amounted to a large island cut through the meadow by three branches of the Black's Fork River. Industrious as ever, the Mormons had replaced the old picket wall with a far more substantial one made of cobblestone masonry, one hundred feet square and fourteen feet high, when they occupied the fort in the early spring of the year. A similar but less substantial wall provided a large corral at the rear of the fort, running along its north wall. The corral was sparsely occupied by a dozen or so horses that lazily browsed on the hay that had been strewn about earlier that morning.

"Yep...thet bunch a skunks beat us, alright. An' here I thought you was gonna outsmart 'em."

Benko Tatum and his gang loitered outside the fort's large south gate. They appeared to be nothing more than a lazy bunch of mountain men passing the time of day by talking with some of the Indian camped near the gate and watching the activities of those entering and leaving the busy post.

"Well...we still might," Obediah said, studying the situation.

"An jest how're we gonna do thet?"

"It sort of appears that Tatum and his cronies think we're going to ride right through that front gate."

"Ain't we? If we're gonna warn them Mormons about what Tatum's gonna do? Thet wall appears mighty substantial, and I don't think we'd get half way up it 'fore Tatum'd find out."

"Maybe we're going to have to warn them some other way, Jasper."

"Huh?"

"Those dudes are watching the front gate," Obediah said. "What if you were to sneak down to that corral and help yourself to a horse while I get out of here and go find Colonel Alexander and warn him?"

"Me?" Jasper hissed. "But that's stealin', ain't it? Around these parts a man can get hisself hung fer such as thet, y' know."

"Well, you're the one without a horse."

"Well...I know, but...yew...."

"You got any better ideas?"

"Well, now...jest how's thet gonna get me int' thet fort? Jest supposin' I don't get shot in the process...huh?

Obediah sat up, stretching his back and looked at his old friend. "It's not going t' get you into the fort," he explained, with exaggerated patience. "It doesn't look to me like you can get into the fort. So, you'll use that cayuse you borrow to go find that bunch you've been raiding us with and warn them. Then, they can tell the rest."

"Umm...," Jasper said, sitting up in the grass, scratching his bristly chin. "Might work."

"You can count on it," Obediah said, sounding a little too confident. Studying the tree line surrounding the meadow, he said, "Go around and come up from the rear, so they can't see you. And if it were me, I'd just walk in and select a horse like I owned the place and ride out the way I came."

Jasper eyed his companion suspiciously. "Thet's how, huh?"

"That's how I'd do it."

"Well, I got some news fer ya, I can figger thet much out fer m'self," Jasper retorted, getting to his feet. "Sometimes yew jest plain.... Where ya goin'?"

"I'm leaving to find Alexander and get the word to him before real trouble starts," Obediah said. "When you get through complaining, you ought to get started, too."

The autumn sun was warm in the bright midday sky as Jasper approached the rear gate of the corral mumbling to himself about looking like he owned the place. As he rounded the corner of the corral's north wall, a man jumped up from a pile of hay near the gate and ran along the high rock wall toward the front of the fort. It was one of Tatum's men, no doubt about it.

"Don't thet spill it?" Jasper mumbled, as he climbed through the pole gate and frantically looked for some sort of bridle. Finding nothing, he walked slowly toward several horses that were bunched in a corner, but the skittish animals scattered and trotted off a few yards. With his eye on a large, sorrel gelding, Jasper slowly herded them back toward the corner, keeping them moving along the wall. As they approached the corner, the wary animals bolted and scattered around the mountain man. Stepping in front of the large sorrel, Jasper grabbed a hand full of its mane and swung himself onto the animal's back as it attempted to dodge past him.

Jasper buried his heels in the horse's flanks yanking its mane to one side, and the animal easily cleared the top of the pole gate. Responding to Jasper's demanding hands and feet, the large animal veered to the right and broke for the wooded hills to the north.

"It's Pughsey!" the man hollered as he rounded the south wall of the fort, his breath coming in short gasps.

"He's...he's...in with the...horses."

"In with the horses?" a startled Benko Tatum yelled, jumping to his feet. "Didn't ya stop 'im, ya dumb coon?"

"Well...he sorta snuck up...I...."

"Sorta snuck up?" he repeated unbelievingly. Infuriated, Benko Tatum struck his unsuspecting compatriot squarely in the side of the face with a roundhouse punch that slammed the man against the rock wall. Bouncing off the wall from the force of the evil blow, the mountain man fell on his face in the dirt at Tatum's feet. "Well don't jest stand there," Tatum raged at the others, "get 'im!"

Mounting their horses, the gang rounded the corner of the fort at full gallop, sending rocks and dust into the air as they spurred the animals into a breakneck race along the narrow trail of slowly settling dust that led into the northern tree line a half mile distant.

Benko waved the gang to a dusty stop in the trees at the top of a low ridge. "That coon couldn't have disappeared this soon," Tatum said, standing in his stirrups and studying the scene before him."

Well...there ain't no other way he came, I'll tell ya that," Will Teeter said, twisting in his saddle and studying their back-trail to the fort in the distance. "This here's the way he came. No doubt about that."

"Yeah...question is where'd 'e go, an' what's 'e gonna do now?" Tatum said, settling in his saddle.

"Ain't no point in tryin' t' find 'im. He's gonna do what we stopped 'im from doing back at the fort."

"Whaddaya mean?" Tatum said, squinting at Teeter.

"He's gonna find some of his Mormon pals an' spill the beans on us, that's what."

"Makes no difference t' me," Tatum said, yanking the reins harshly over his horse's neck, urging it back the way they had come. "All it means is we better get movin' an' get there first. Let's go."

Less than five days later, after a hard ride east, Jasper Pughsey rode over a small rise at full gallop and reined his lathering horse to a dusty stop before Major Lot Smith at the head of a small column.

"Trouble's brewin', Major," Jasper said, dismounting. "An' lots of it."

Lot Smith turned in his saddle and said, "Sergeant Teasdale, we'll make temporary camp here. Have cook prepare the evening meal, and be ready to move out in a couple of hours."

Smith dismounted and led his horse away from the confusion of the temporary bivouac preparations. "Trouble's all I've seen, Pughsey, and you're here to tell me something I don't know?"

"Well, you ain't gonna like it. I'll garntee thet much."

"Well...out with it, man," the Major said, leading his horse to a large rock and sitting down. "I can always use some bad news before I eat."

"Then...this oughta give ya a real appetite," Jasper said. "First off, there's a big wagon train back a ways...a bunch of 'em."

"Where are they, Jasper?"

"I figger ma'be twenty miles back...not much more 'n thet."

"Where, exactly?"

Jasper sat down on a large rock and squinted up at the younger man. "They're on the old Mormon road...near Sandy Fork," he replied, rubbing the small of his back. "Looks t' me like they're headin' fer Ham's Fork, ma'be...at least not Fort Bridger."

"Back hurtin', old timer?" the Major grinned.

"Not so's you'd notice, an' whaddaya mean, 'old timer'?" Jasper responded, irritably.

"I guess Rockwell was wrong after all. It's getting so you can't trust anybody anymore."

"What 'd he tell ya?"

"He sold me and General Wells a bill of goods on your scouting abilities, but maybe you're more ready for a rocking chair than a scout's horse."

"Why, I ain't seen many a you fancy pants young'ns I couldn't out ride, out scout, out fight...."

"Out lie," Smith said, a good-natured grin splitting his friendly face.

The past weeks of tracking and following the slowly advancing army had been difficult, frustrating work. But in their brief encounters, the two men had quickly learned to respect one another's abilities. Lot Smith was a thoroughly professional soldier, and he had a talent for tactical thinking that inevitably gave his small, ill-equipped band full advantage in nearly every situation they had encountered.

Though Jasper Pughsey had reluctantly accepted the request that he scout for Smith, preferring to work on his own or in association with Porter Rockwell, the mountain man had quickly grown to respect the younger man's abilities, and he especially appreciated someone that proved to be a quick learner. Lot Smith was nothing, if not a quick learner. To the mountain man's great discomfort, what Smith learned the quickest and seemed to enjoy the most was jerking on Jasper Pughsey's rope, and he had soon discovered where all of the old scout's sore spots were.

"Well...jest lemme lay this'n on ya then," Pughsey said, grabbing his horse's reins and heading toward the makeshift camp where the rag-tag Mormon force was lining up for its evening meal. "They's some what gets edjacated slower 'n others...an' harder."

"You figure as much, huh?" Smith said, following the cantankerous old mountain man.

"Yep...more'n anything, you remind me a Obediah Jones. Why, a more snot-nosed young'n was never borne of woman, an' it was left almost entirely t' me ta edjacate 'im, too."

"Almost entirely?"

"Yep...a few years back...me an' Bug's Boys," Jasper said, tethering his horse with some of the others. "An' a fine job I did, too, if I do say so m'self. Wagh!"

The men moved aside as Lot Smith followed Jasper up to the cook fire. "Bug's Boys?"

"Yep...Bug's Boys," Jasper snickered, taking great

enjoyment from Smith's apparent ignorance. "Why, I don't know what woulda happened to Obediah if I hadn't saved 'is bacon on more'n one occasion."

"Bug's Boys," Lot repeated, contemplatively.

"Seems like I'm gonna have t' do as much fer you...as if I ain't called on t' do enough already."

"Well...who in tarnation are Bug's Boys?"

Jasper chuckled to himself, and said, "An' here I been thinkin' yew Mormons had all the answers, an' yew don't even know who ol' Bug is."

"Well...we've got a few answers that just might surprise you, but I'll admit your 'Old Bug' has to be a new one—on me, at least."

"Now, why don't that surprise me none?" Jasper mumbled.

"What?"

"Nothin'."

"Well then, who in tarnation is he? And if you're such an all-fired good teacher, where's this Obediah Jones fellow now, anyway?"

"Smell them beans, boy?" Jasper said, as one of the camp cooks slopped a huge, steaming spoon-full of the pasty, brown collation onto his tin plate. "I can't be expected ta expend energy on edjacatin' the likes of yew without some victuals."

"Well...these beans will do the likes of you some good, Pughsey. They've been blessed at every meal."

"These the same ones?" Jasper said, squinting more closely at his plate.

"Yep...they've been blessed so many times, cook just refers to them as Blessed Beans. Take your fill."

"Yer tellin' me? I've sat with a growlin', empty meat bag

through many a them blessin's," Jasper said, testing a hot spoon full. "If these beans ain't holy by now, they ain't never gonna be."

Their plates full, the two men moved around the chuck wagon and sat down in the scarce shade it provided from the late afternoon sun.

"Ya know, Pughsey," the Major said, his mouth full of the tasty beans and pork belly, "you remind me of my grandmother. It never failed, she...."

"Yer what...?"

"Yep...my grandmother. Like you, at your advanced age, she was none too easy to look at either, though I loved her more than words can say."

"At my advanced...."

"Yep." The major pulled a long strip of meat from his beans and ate it with contemplation. "But, I could never get a straight answer out of her...at least not until she got something out of me. Usually a lot of work...on the end of a broom...or a mop...or something else equally repugnant to a growing boy."

"Repug...."

"Means nasty."

"I know what it means," Jasper responded with irritation. "Now, yew looky here, ya...."

"And then, when I got it, it usually was half story and half something else. Why she...."

"Oh, yeah...well. Let me tell you somethin' mister, what you get from me yew generally can't get along without. An' knowin' about Bug's Boys is one of them facts related t' your survival. So yew better listen up."

Well, now," Lot Smith said, looking up from his half-empty plate, "I'm paying real close attention. Who in tarnation are Bug's Boys?"

"Mister, ol' Bug is the devil."

"The Devil?" Smith said, with some surprise. "You mean Satan?"

"Yep...Old Scratch hisself...an' no other. An' the injuns...whaddaya call em?"

"Lamanites?"

"Yeah...well...they's Bugs's Boys. In particular, the Blackfeet. They's the Devil's children, pure and true, an' many's the dust-up I had with 'em, me an Obediah Jones."

Jasper began to warm to his story with mounting enthusiasm. "Why, I remember oncet, me an Obediah was...."

"Well, if you taught 'im so well, where is this Jones fella? I could surely use such a man right now."

"He's warnin' the army?"

"Warning the army?" Smith said, setting down his empty plate.

"Yep...but thanks t' me, that Obediah was some. He's got the h'ar of the b'ar in 'im, sure."

"What army?"

"Well now, jest what army d' you think?" Jasper retorted, knowing he had turned the tables on Lot Smith. Scratching his bristly, grizzled chin, he said, "Yew, too. Someday, ma'be, if ya...."

"Me, too what?"

"You'll ketch on, stedda thinkin' yer s' smart," Jasper said, loudly scraping the remaining beans from his plate.

"Sometimes learning's a two-way street," Lot broke in, getting to his feet and dusting off the seat of his pants. "I know you learned that much in the mountains all these years."

"Whadda ya mean?" Jasper, said squinting up at the Major.

"It's not only the Blackfeet...."

Whaddaya mean by thet?"

"We're up against Bug's Boys again, as far as I'm concerned. These troops we're moving against are doing the Devil's work as surely as any evil has ever been done."

"Yeah, and they ain't the only ones, neither."

"Now, what is thet supposed to mean?" Lot Smith said, mocking the old mountain man.

"Yew ever heard of Benko Tatum?" Jasper asked, getting to his feet.

The Major studied the old mountain man's face. "Can't say as I have. Should I?"

"Well, if you ain't, you're surely gonna."

"Who's Benko Tatum?" Smith asked hesitantly, in an effort to cover the apprehension in his voice. The guerrilla fighter knew that what he was about to hear from his scout meant nothing but trouble, and he knew that is what all of this give and take had been leading up to.

"Tatum's a bald-headed snake thet's been tryin' t' pass hisself off as a mountain man fer as long as I been out in these mountains," Jasper said with a gesture. Why, he's..."

"That long, huh?"

"...he's...I," Jasper sputtered. "Now, yeu jest better looky here, this feller's pure p'ison," he said, stifling a groan as he rose from his place near the wagon's wheel.

"Sorry."

"He ain't nothin' t' full with, and him an' his gang's gonna get this shootin' war started, less'n we can stop 'im first."

"How many of them are there?"

"There's him an' five of his footlickin' toadeaters."

"And just how are six men going to start this war?"

"Oh...my stars," Jasper said, with an ostentatious groan. "With all I gotta do, I still have ta help ya through the simplest thinkin'."

"Oh...well, now...I...."

"Jest suppose," Jasper said, exhibiting a lofty patience, "when we get close t' thet army yer s' concerned about, somebody starts takin' some shots and knocks a few of these fellers outta their saddles, jest suppose," he said, waving his hand at the small band of men cleaning up after their evening meal. "An' jest suppose it's made t' look like we're gonna get shot up pretty bad, jest suppose—lots a widow-makin' goin' on, huh? Now, you an' me both know we ain't supposed t' do no bodily harm, accordin' t' brother Brigham. But...on the other hand, we cain't jest set by an' get ourselves killed, can we? So, Mr. Major, whadda ya gonna do...jest suppose?"

"Pughsey," Smith said, with equally feigned patience, "anyone every told you just how purely irritating you can be—jest suppose?"

"An' then suppose," Jasper continued unperturbed, knowing he truly had the best of this young whippersnapper, "the army starts takin' a few hot balls in the backs of a few troopers, huh? Whaddaya suppose their gonna do, huh?"

"So, that's their plan?" Lot Smith said, squatting down beside the wagon. "Where do you think they 'll hit us?"

Jasper sat down next to the Major and leaned back against the wheel of the chuck wagon. "Well...it's gotta be somewhere around Fort Bridger, or maybe Echo Canyon. But they gotta do it fast, whether it's dawned on 'em 'r not, winter's gonna close in one of these days. Jest feel this air.

"He's dangerous, Lot. Thet skunk's tried to put me an' Obediah Jones under fer years. This is as much about me an Obediah Jones as it is about anything."

"How do you think they figure to benefit? By just killing the two of you?"

"Nope, they want them army supplies, or as much as they can get."

"Supplies," the Major said, with surprise. "What do they want all that stuff for."

"Major...there's a big market fer thet kinda stuff back in the Kansas Territory, and there's a lot a war talk goin' on back in the states."

"Somehow, we've got to get word to the leader of that forward group of troops."

"No need. You was askin' about Obediah Jones? He's been scoutin' fer 'em, and he knows the plan. He'll get the word to 'em. Best we turn around an' head back fer Fort Bridger."

The wooden camp chair squeaked, as Colonel Alexander leaned back and contemplated the tall mountain man standing before him. "Well, Mr. Jones, be that as it may, it changes nothing."

"Changes nothing? Colonel, you can't...."

"Indeed I can, and I will. My orders are explicit, Mr. Jones. I am to move this army into Great Salt Lake City, and I intend to do it against Mormons or against Benko Tatum and his gang of thugs, or anyone else."

"I understand your orders, Colonel Alexander," Obediah argued, "but just how do you expect these Mormon guerrillas to respond when Tatum and his men start the shooting? They are going to start firing back—at us. And then what?"

"Mr. Jones, let me remind you that you are my scout, not my tactician," Alexander responded irritably. "My men will be placed on alert, and they will respond with hostile and deadly fire, regardless of who starts the shooting. Is that clear?"

"It's more than clear, I'm afraid."

"Good," the officer said, attempting to rise as he moved from his desk near the wall of the tent. "Now, this encampment is going to be a fairly permanent one. We may have to endure the winter here at Hams Fork, since the Mormons have inhabited Fort Bridger, and we can expect no understanding from them. Therefore, what I want of you is to...."

"Beggin' the Colonel's pardon, sir." Sergeant O'Riley's voice came from just outside the tent.

"What is it, Sergeant?"

O'Riley entered the tent, and wiped his large, red face with his handkerchief. When it was his dreaded responsibility to convey bad news to his Colonel, his face drooped and crinkled as if he were about to burst into tears. It was a sight that brought no end of pleasure to all who knew him.

"Beggin' the Colonel's pardon, sir, but I ain't never seen the likes a the man what jest brought this here packet t' the Colonel," O'Riley, said, handing a large leather folder to Alexander.

"Well...what does he want?"

"Beggin' yer pardon, sir, he didn't say. Just said this here was from a General Wells, sir. Said he'd wait, sir, 'e did."

"General Wells?" Alexander asked. "Who's General Wells?"

"He's the senior man leading the Mormons," Obediah responded, moving the tent flap aside. "And that's Orrin Porter Rockwell out there."

"Place him under arrest," Alexander said, motioning to a hesitant O'Riley.

"I wouldn't do that, Colonel," Obediah said, studying the scene outside the tent. "Seems he came under a white flag, and..."

"That he did, sir," O'Riley said with emphasis.

"...and if half the stories I heard about him are true, if you did get him under arrest, you probably couldn't keep him there—at least not without someone getting hurt," Obediah said. "Besides, he's not alone. There's another one back in the trees," Obediah said, studying the tree line. "I know that fella, too. Another mountain man by the name of Marrianne, as I recall," Obediah said, letting the tent flap fall into place. "And there might just be more."

Opening the pouch Alexander said, "You have an irritating admiration for these confounded Mormons, Jones."

"I'm sorry you find it so troublesome, sir."

"Well...that tears it," the Colonel said, scanning the documents in his hands. "There seems to be no end to the arrogance of that so-called Mormon Prophet. Look at this," he said, handing one of the papers to Obediah, "and talk of peace to me now, Jones. A proclamation...invading Utah Territory, indeed," he huffed. "I'm afraid there is little alternative now."

Alexander snatched the document back before Obediah could finish reading. "Just look here," he said, jabbing the paper with his finger. "'I now further direct that you retire forthwith from the territory, by the same route you entered. Should you deem this impracticable, and prefer to remain until spring in the vicinity of your present encampment, Black's Fork, or Green River, you can do so in peace and unmolested, on condition that you deposit your arms and ammunition with....' Can you believe the arrogance of the man?" Alexander said, his voice rising as he waved the document at Jones and O'Riley.

"What else could we have expected?" Obediah Jones asked.

"Compliance with the law," Alexander hollered, "that's what I expect, and I will settle for nothing less."

The angry Colonel returned to his camp table and began to write. When he finished he waved the letter at O'Riley, and said, "Give that messenger this, and tell him to tell his General Wells," pronouncing the word "General" with obvious contempt, "that I have received his communication; tell him that I have established a permanent encampment known as Camp Winfield, and that we are here to stay; tell him that I will enter the Salt Lake Valley as ordered at the earliest possible time; and tell Mr. Jones' fearsome Mormon friend to get the word to Young that he had best recant and consider the well-being of his people before that of his own pride. Is that clear?"

"It is, indeed, sir," the red faced Sergeant said, snapping to attention before his commanding officer.

"Then, tell him!"

Sergeant O'Riley folded the letter and turned from his commanding officer's desk with a proper military snap. "I'll tell 'im, sir."

"No...wait," Alexander said, slumping back in his camp

chair. "Tear that up, Sergeant, and I'll prepare a somewhat less strident response." He leaned forward and picked up his pen, pulling some paper from the drawer beneath the table. "Go summon my senior officers, and tell the messenger to report to his commanding officer that I have received the communication, and an appropriate response will be forthcoming."

"May I, sir?" Obediah asked.

"Do it, Jones, and O'Riley tell my officers to assemble immediately. And Jones...."

"Colonel?"

"I want you to scout the entire area between here and Echo Canyon. I want to know where every Mormon in the field is, where their camps are, where their fortifications are, and what their movements seem to be. I want to know the exact strength of Fort Bridger, in terms of men, forage, guns, whatever. In short, I want to know everything you can find out about the enemy."

Obediah lifted the tent flap to leave, but before he could step from the tent, the Colonel said, "When you return I want you and my staff to prepare a detailed map and a plan for entering Great Salt Lake City under hostile conditions. Any questions?"

"None. Except...," Obediah said tentatively.

"Then leave now, and return as quickly as possible."

It was after midnight and cold, and the voices of the drunken teamsters could be heard from the dying fires that slowly danced and fluttered between two rows of wagons carelessly hidden in the shallow gully below.

Jasper studied the encampment carefully, confidence

rising within him that the skinners, whoever they were, could be easily subdued. Unlike the encampments of the invading army, this one had been given little thought, and the advantage clearly lay with him and Lot Smith's guerrillas. It was dark, it was cold, and the men below were obviously drunk.

Major Lot Smith and his small force were hidden in the blackness of a small stand of pinion, juniper, and scrub brush not far from where they had suspected the wagon train to have stopped for the night.

Jasper's form appeared unexpectedly at Smith's side. "Appears there's abou..."

"Damn and tarnation," Smith yelped, yanking his revolver from its holster.

Jasper sat down at the base of a large juniper tree, disappearing in the darkness. "Well now, Major, somethin' botherin' ya?" He made no attempt at hiding his delight at spooking the younger commander.

"Sneaking up on a man like that can get a body killed, y' know," Smith responded huffily.

"So can relaxin' too much in a place like this," Jasper said, his pedantic tone calculated to further nettle his friend. "In the dark, not bein' heard is not bein' seen."

"Pughsey, you are...."

"Twenty-six of 'em, I calcalate."

"Twenty-six what?"

"Wagons. Twenty-six in two rows...with three camp fires twixt 'em. But, Lot, we ain't got time fer this kinda thing, easy as it looks t' be."

"Jasper, this is exactly why we're here," Lot Smith hissed, peering in the darkness at his scout, "and we're not going to leave this train in one piece. Right now, I don't care about Tatum. We'll get the word back alright, but right now we can put some hurt to these invaders."

"But I tell ya, we got us some warnin' t' do quick-like, not raidin'," Jasper urged.

Ignoring the mountain man's protest, Lot Smith said, "There's probably one teamster for each wagon, and if you throw in eight or ten extra men...probably forty or so men. Let's pay them a visit," Smith said, mounting his horse, and urging it back among the small force hidden in the moonless night.

"Now...jest a minute," Jasper said, scrambling from under the juniper. "You...."

Explaining the situation to his men, Lot Smith turned in the saddle, and said, "We ease up on them, men, and take them by surprise. Remember no one...them or us...is to get hurt."

The guerilla leader nudged his horse toward the enemy encampment. "This way, Sergeant Teasdale, in a column of twos—and quietly, please."

Jasper eased his horse next to Smith's as the enemy encampment appeared in the wide, shallow gully below them.

Lot Smith stood in his stirrups. "Why, man...there are more than twenty-six wagons down there," he hissed. "Twice that...."

"Well, thet's what I tried t' tell ya," Jasper shot back. "Twenty-six in two rows."

"Why didn't ya tell me two rows of twenty six each?"

"Thet is what I told ya."

"There are twice as many men down there as we calculated. We can't...."

"Why not?" Jasper said, warming to the challenge and

forgetting Benko Tatum's threat.

"It's too risky. They could overpower us, and I have explicit orders not to get anyone hurt—them or us."

"Wagh!" Jasper spat. "Jest like I said...I always gotta learn ya."

"What?" Lot smith, said angrily. "Why...."

"Look behind us. How many men we got?"

"We've got twenty."

"Can yew see 'em all?"

"Well...of course not, it...."

Lot Smith hated nothing more than being bested by Jasper Pughsey. On anything. But most of all he hated getting caught short in this kind of situation.

Jasper Pughsey was the first to break the grudging silence. "Now, if we was t' get a few men in a line an' advance on that encampment, with the rest strung out behind us in the darkness, why we...."

"Damnation," Major Smith said, half under his breath.

"What's thet yew was sayin'?"

"Nothing." The Major responded, as he quickly gave the orders to advance. "And remember...I do the talking."

"Where's another bottle?" the lurching teamster asked his companion, slouched against a wagon wheel. Too much whisky made the wagons and the other men sort of liquid as the dying fires caused the shadows to dance and fold around them. "I said wh...."

His pie-eyed companion followed his blinking, unsteady stare.

"Evening," Major Lot Smith said, steadying his nervous horse.

Trying to focus on this intruder and the buckskin-clad rider at his left, the teamster saw the other mounted men—countless, woozy numbers of them strung out into the swimming darkness.

"Where'd you come...an'...who the devil are ya?"

"Where is the captain of this train?" Smith asked, as other unsteady revelers began drifting toward them.

"Who...whaddaya want, anyways?"

"I have some difficult business to discuss with him," Smith said, patiently. "Now, go get him before I lose my patience."

A big man stepped from behind the nearest wagon, tucking his shirt into his pants. "I'm the boss here," he said, steadily. "An' you haven't answered 'is question. Who are ya and whaddaya want?"

Sitting next to Lot Smith, Jasper Pughsey studied the wagon boss. He was big and obviously tough. Unlike his companions, he did not appear to be drunk. Recognizing that the situation could quickly get out of hand, Jasper dismounted and moved around between his horse and that of Lot Smith.

Sensing the tension, Smith dismounted and walked up to the man, his hand out. "I'm Lot Smith, and I'd like to talk some business with you."

The big man warily took his hand. "John M. Dawson, wagon master for the firm of Russell, Majors, and Waddell. Now, what is it ya want t' talk about under these conditions?"

"Well, sir. I'm Major Lot Smith of the First Battalion of Cavalry, Nauvoo Legion, and I...."

"Nauvoo Legi...what in tarnation is the Nau...?"

"What I want to talk to you about is burning your

wagons," Lot said, pleasantly.

"Burn my wa...."

"That is correct, sir. Now, if you'll just have your men remove their private property from the wagons as quickly as possible, my men here," he said, waving his hand at the darkness to his rear, "mean to put a little fire into them."

"For God's sake, you can't burn the trains!" the man responded hotly.

"It is precisely for His sake that I am going to burn them," the Major responded matter-of-factly. "Now, have your men stack their arms back there beyond the wagons and assemble over there near Mr. Pughsey, our scout— where they won't get hurt."

Smith motioned Jasper Pughsey forward. "If everyone remains calm and does as they're told, no one will get hurt, and we will be quickly on our way."

"Now...look here, Smith...or whatever yer name is, you just can't...."

"Mr. Dawson, look around you," the Major abruptly interjected. "You, sir, are in no position to try to dictate terms or to interfere. You and your men are combatants invading the Territory of Utah against conditions laid down by its governor. You are supplying an invading army with the materials necessary for its dirty work, and that places you and your men in the most grave danger—where you now stand, sir."

"But...you...we...."

The bluff was working. And as the wagon boss seemed to realize the hopelessness of his position, faced with an obviously insurmountable force surrounding his wagons in the darkness, his self-confidence and belligerence began to sputter as Lot Smith's took flight.

"Sergeant Teasdale...make sure the men of the battalion keep their mounts well back from the wagons."

"Men of the batal...." Dawson's breath drained from his body.

Teasdale spurred his horse from the head of the column, and disappeared back into the darkness. His gruff voice could be heard clearly in the cold night air as he hollered, "All you men stay alert, now! The fireworks 'r about to start!"

"We want none of these men to be needlessly harmed," Smith said, remounting his horse. "Mr. Dawson, assemble your men back away from those two wagons, and have them—carefully, now—stack their arms." Twisting in his saddle, he hollered into the darkness, "Sergeant, two guards up front, please! We don't want anyone wandering off."

"You're not going to leave us out here unarmed, man?"

"That is up to you, sir. Cooperate, and you have nothing to fear from us," Smith said, nudging his horse so close that his boot pressed into Dawson's chest. "Now...tell me, sir. What have you on board these wagons?"

"Well...," he said, backing away from Smith's intimidating boot, "...I guess I have a bill of...."

"You guess? You had better, and you may wish to get it, sir," Smith said, again nudging his horse up to the now frightened wagon boss. "My boys are much in need of overcoats and other supplies, the season is getting late and the weather cold. And, as you can plainly tell, we'll need a goodly number."

Again the man backed away, and again the horse moved to press Smith's boot against the now thoroughly intimidated man whose back was pressed uncomfortably against the nearest wagon.

"Oh...and also, Mr. Dawson," Smith said, pressing a little harder. "Would there be any powder on these wagons? If so, I'll have to ask you to set fire to each wagon yourself. We wouldn't want any of my boys to get hurt in the blast, would we?"

"If I...here," the man said, withdrawing a worn leather pouch from the pocket of his shabby, cotton pants. "You can see fer...."

Refusing the pouch, Lot said, "Best you check it yourself, Mr. Dawson. It will be your honor to set a fine blaze.

"Well...now...I ain't right sure, but I think there's some...saltpetre and sulphur in the wagons."

Lot Smith looked at the man in mock surprise. "Now, wouldn't that make a bang? Mr. Pughsey?" he said, looking around. "Fire up a torch for Mr. Dawson, here"

Disappearing briefly into the darkness, the mountain man quickly reappeared with a tar-coated torch and thrust the handle of the blackened staff at the frightened wagon boss.

"Jest light it right over there," Jasper said, nodding his head to the nearest dying fire.

Reflexively the man took the torch, his eyes darting between his two tormentors. "Oh...now...for the good Lord's sake, don't make me. I've been sick, and I'm not well yet. I don't want t' be hurt."

Major Smith eased the pressure on Dawson's chest and took the torch from him. Leaning down, his face threateningly close to Dawson's, he said, "Take some of your men and fetch us some provisions from these wagons. And," he said, emphasizing each word with a nudge of the torch handle, "be generous, and don't try anything stupid."

Jasper Pughsey took the man by the arm, and in mock confidence whispered loudly, "Get plenty a sugar and coffee. Mostly...these Mormons here," he said, nodding his head toward Lot Smith, "don't use coffee—kinda short-sighted— but we don't want them army troopers enjoyin' it neither."

As Jasper gave the man a shove toward the men under guard, Smith looked at the captive skinners and said loudly, "Make no mistake, Dawson...any attempt to escape or interfere, and not a one of you culprits will be left alive."

Lot Smith wheeled his horse around and hollered into the darkness, "Sergeant Teasdale, send Big James forward."

Jasper Pughsey watched closely as the pile of contraband from the wagons grew and then diminished as the goods were dispersed down the line of Mormon troopers into the darkness. "Now that's right efficient, Mr. Dawson," he said to the defeated train boss.

"That's right, sir," Lot Smith said, joining the two. "As this material gets distributed to all of my men out there," he said, his hand sweeping the darkness beyond the light of the camp fires, "you can rest assured of their eternal gratitude. And, you can rest assured also, sir, of its efficient use in preventing the unwarranted invasion of which you and the rest of these mongrel ne'er-do-wells seem intent upon."

"Now...jest a darn minute, Major. My men and...."

"Save your breath, Mr. Dawson, because the fun is about to begin," Smith said, as a huge bear of a man joined them. "Jasper, I want you and Big James, here, to fire the wagons."

"'ppears like this feller could fire 'em hisself," Jasper Pughsey said, with an appraising glance at the big man.

"True enough, Mr. Pughsey," Smith chuckled," but there is something poetic, a kind of military justice, in you two Gentiles putting the torch to a Gentile train—Gentiles spoiling Gentiles, so to speak."

"Well...now, this ain't no time ta.... What in tarnation is a 'Gentile', anyways?"

"You and Big James, here, are Gentiles."

"Now...jest a minute, here," Jasper said, with some force, "I ain't no Gentile."

"Yes you are. Furthermore, so are the rest of these heathen," Lot Smith said, nodding toward their prisoners.

"Why...man, I...."

"This isn't the time or the place to discuss it, Jasper. We've got work to do...and then there's Tatum to...."

"Well, you was the one who...."

"Big James, here, is as Irish as Murphy's pig, aren't ya soldier?"

"Indeed I am, sir, an' I still have a love of the sod burnin' within me these many years, now."

"Talkative, ain't 'e," Jasper muttered. "On top of that," Lot said, seemingly putting the argument to rest. "He's as Catholic as the Pope, or at least as most true Irishmen would own up t' being. Ain't that right, Big James?"

"Well, I ain't none a them things," Jasper said, his anger rising, "and don't this seem like a dumb place fer this kind a palaver?"

"See? Neither one of you are members of the Church, so you're Gentiles."

"Yew mean if I...." Jasper began, mounting his horse.

"That's right. If you were, God would take you under his wing and you'd see things considerably different. Now, light those torches and let's get it done."

"Yew...oh, common 'Gentile,'" Jasper said with some disgust. "Let's get t' making life miserable fer the rest a these here other Gentiles."

CHAPTER TEN

Huddled in their heavy buffalo skin coats, Benko Tatum and Will Teeter leaned over the horns of their saddles and watched from a thick stand of cedar and pinion as two men made their way down separate rows of wagons setting their torches to each. Throughout the night the wind had picked up and blew with a cold persistence that soon had each wagon fully ablaze.

"So...it starts," Teeter said.

"They done some b'fore, but this here's a even prettier sight," Tatum chuckled.

"More'n these been burned?"

"Two 'r three trains, but not this close to the army camp, nor so much stuff," Tatum said, each word surrounded with puffs of white in the numbing air. "When Alexander finds out this here train's been hit, he's gonna be madder'n a grisly with a sore tooth—an' that's jest what we been waitin' fer."

"Mad 'r not, right now I'd like t' be a little closer t' that fire. I keep fergettin' just how cold this country can get."

"You bet," Tatum chuckled, "and that's gonna make things all the better fer us. Nothin' can shorten a feller's fuse like bein' cold'n miserable, and everything goin' up in flames down there's gonna make life a pure misery fer them what has t' do without—thanks t' them thievin' Mormons. Now's the time fer us t' start movin'."

"Why? What ya got in mind?"

"Let's get back t' the hut," Tatum said, reining his horse around and starting down the backside of the sparsely

151

wooded hill. "We'll roust out the others and be back here before dawn."

Teeter's horse trotted alongside Tatum's. "An' then what?" Teeter asked.

"Look for our chance," Tatum responded, as the two men disappeared into the night. "Under the right circumstance, three 'r four well-placed shots could get the party started fer real."

At first the snow fell lightly, a flake here and there, but as the blackness of the night began to fade in the east, the wind died and the clouds lowered. The snow, which began with such a lack of promise, soon built with intensity, covering the ground around the smoldering wagons with what quickly became a thick blanket of white. Then the wind began, and the blowing snow hissed across the ground and built into deep drifts wherever it met with some obstruction.

A column of troopers paused at the top of a near-by hill overlooking the scene of the Mormon raid. The platoon leader, a young Lieutenant, left the front of the column and trotted forward to get a better look at the skeletal remains of the still smoldering supply train.

"Damnation," he muttered, turning in his saddle. "Sergeant...send four men forward to search for anything of value," he hollered, the wind carrying his voice away.

Four men passed at a fast gallop, and the Sergeant reined in beside him.

"Seems they did a pretty complete job, sir."

"Seems they did, Sergeant—very thorough. We have a desperate need for what was on that wagon train."

The wind buffeted the two soldiers as, hunched in their long coats, they watched the men kick around in the burned wreckage.

The Lieutenant wheeled his horse around. "Call 'em back, Sergeant," he said, twisting in his saddle and looking back at the four below. "No point in freezing, and there's nothing down there but cinders."

The two trotted back toward the remainder of the column, and were soon joined by the other four.

"Nothin' left, sir," one of the troopers said, reining in next to the officer and Sergeant. "Just charcoal."

"Back in formation, men," the Sergeant said, waving the men on. "What now, sir?"

"What now?" the officer snapped. "Disaster's what's now, Sergeant."

"Ain't nobody lookin' forward t' this winter, sir. Seems like it's just gonna get longer an' longer."

"Turn 'em around, Sergeant. We need to report back as quickly as possible," the young Lieutenant said, spurring his horse. "This storm is getting worse by the minute."

At the head of their somewhat disheveled column of victorious but exhausted Mormon guerrillas, Lot Smith and Jasper Pughsey leaned into the bitter wind as their horses, ice accumulating in their winter hair, struggled through the deepening snow.

With the collapse of the first wagon in a shower of hot sparks and flames, the small band had felt the stimulation of a substantial victory. The invaders had been denied tons of urgently needed war supplies, and for the first time Lot Smith's small band felt a welcome surge of confidence from the knowledge that they could stop the army in its tracks. But with the freezing wind and thickening snow, their enthusiasm soon began to dwindle. And as the storm built into the first terrible mountain blizzard of the season, their bodies reacted to the biting cold with the same intense pain felt by their adversaries.

"Best we find someplace t' hole-up, Major," Jasper shouted at the man next to him, his voice quickly becoming lost in the blinding gale. "Least 'till this lets up some."

Lot Smith, his face lost where his greatcoat and his hat came together, nodded in response, and the column moved to the lee side of a steep mountain slope. Above them, the thinly pine-clad shoulder of the mountain broke into a sheer cliff that dropped to a wide, rock-strewn gully floor and offered the hope of some protection from the intensifying blizzard.

At several places along the edge of the cliff a number of old Yellow Pine trees had lost their tenuous grip and had fallen over, their exposed roots still struggling for life in the cracks of the bare rock at the top, their bows supporting their weight on the gully floor below. Numberless summer floods had piled the mountain's refuse against these toppled giants, and now each formed a natural lean-to beneath which some shelter and relief from the storm could be sought. Men and horses alike crowded into these meager sanctuaries, each taking warmth from the other.

"I hate to say this Pughsey, but we've got to get word to General Wells about the wagon train and about your friend Tatum's treachery," Lot Smith said, blowing into his numb hands. "Got any suggestions?"

"'Course I do. You better go now," Jasper said, huddling against the cold rock face of the cliff.

"Well...as usual, old timer...you've got things confused," the guerilla leader said, nudging his friend. "Probably the storm, what with the cold and your advanced age and all...."

"Well," Jasper replied, huddling deeper into his coat and slumping to the ground, "what with my age 'an all...surely you ain't sayin' I should go. Huh?"

Lot Smith squatted down next to the mountain man and leaned against the cold rock. "Well...see, it's like this. I'm the commander of this here outfit, and you're the scout."

"Mm," Jasper grunted, slapping his legs to restore some feeling, and trying to sound thoughtful. "Kinda the...way I figgered it...too."

"Well...then you can see...."

"Wagh!" Jasper snorted, rising from his cold, cramped position. "Talkin' t' yew's more tiresome than this here blizzard. "I might jest mosey, 'an see if'n I can find m'self more sociable company."

Looking up at the half-frozen scout, Lot Smith started to rise.

"Yew jest stay put," Jasper said, nudging Lot back against the rock. "I...."

"Oh, I wasn't going to say anything, except...."

"Except nothin'," Jasper said, attempting to free his horse from the tight tangle of men and animals. "Serious times call fer serious doin's, an' thet takes a man, not a boy".

"You be careful, you hear!" Lot hollered, as Jasper Pughsey mounted his horse and disappeared into the blizzard.

* * *

"We ain't goin' out in this," Teeter said, turning from the small window of the low, dark trapper's hut and returning to the fire that burned hot in the rock fireplace. "Ain't man nor beast that could survive out there."

"Ain't gonna survive, if we don't let 'em," Tatum growled. "This is just the kinda weather t' impart some real misery. Question is, who's man enough among us t' do it."

"Ain't no need."

Tatum turned on the man as he climbed down from the low loft. "What'd you say, Jenks?" he growled.

"I jest meant that there probably ain't nobody out in this storm, man ner beast, Benko. That's all."

"Did ya, now?" Benko said, with a mean edge to his voice. "Well, maybe we're just gonna go out an' see," he said, giving the man a nasty poke. "Them troopers was out there wasn't they? Huh?"

"Benko, we...."

"Shut up, Teeter. I'm tellin' ya all, now's the time t' get things riled up. Not when the sun's shinin' an' everybody's happy, ya dumb bunch a...."

"Awright...then," Teeter said, angrily. "If yer sa set on this, let's go."

"Get yer stuff, Jenks. You an' me an' Teeter, here's, gonna scout that army encampment an' see what we can find. An' if that patrol ain't back yet, we jest might drop one'r two of 'im in the snow," Tatum said, struggling into his coat. "Where's them other two?"

"Left," Jenks mumbled.

"What'd you say?" Benko snarled.

"I said, they left, Benko," Jenks said, apologetically.

"Whaddaya mean, they left?"

"They jest left, Benko. Said they was tired, is all."

"Get yer possibles," Tatum said, shoving Jenks toward the door. "If you let 'em go, you can carry their load. Let's get at it."

Jasper's horse lunged through the deep snow to the top of the ridgeline, and the mountain man peered intently into the blizzard. The narrow valley before him was nearly concealed with a dense shroud of blowing white, the thick pine forest on the opposite slope barely visible.

As he began urging his nearly frozen mount down the steep, thinly timbered slope, from the corner of his eye the mountain man thought he saw a more dense puff of white appear. With shocking recognition he was suddenly and violently knocked from his saddle and slammed to the steep snow-covered earth, the deep unmistakable thump of a rifle shot reverberating off the surrounding hills.

The force of the unexpected blow threw him headlong down the precipitous mountain side and he plunged through the wind-blown powder and over a rock outcropping to a hard ledge below. Stunned and only half conscious, Jasper staggered to his feet with the realization that he had been shot, and he somehow had little doubt by whom. That he had to get away was the single thought in his paralyzed mind as he struggled through the snow, leaving only his hat and a trail of blood to mark the spot where he fell.

Teeter slowly lowered his Hawken and blew at the smoking muzzle. A vicious grin spread across face.

"That oughta put that old pork eater outta the picture," he snorted.

"If that was Pughsey, he ain't no pork eater. That kinda thinkin' can make a man dead," Benko Tatum hissed. "Don't count that old coon out 'till ya see him put under. An' even then don't trust what ya see."

The three men made their way slowly down the thickly wooded northwest slope of the narrow valley, their horses lunging through the snow causing the deep powder to hiss and tumble before them.

"Where'd 'e go?" Jenks hollered. "You can bet he's dead. Why don't we jest leave 'im?"

"He fell offa that ledge over yonder and disappeared on the other side," Teeter shouted. "Benko's right, we gotta find 'em."

"What fer? If 'e ain't dead, he's gonna freeze—if 'e don't bleed t' death first. You got 'im square," Jenks insisted.

"Shut up...Jenks," Tatum shrieked, twisting in his saddle. "If you ain't up t' this then go on back and squat by the fire, ya squaw!"

A short, thin, weasel-like man with a sharp prominent nose and close-set eyes that seemed to be constantly shifting, Jenks was not the most forceful of creatures, and like most of his desperate kind, he was a coward. But like all innate cowards, he harbored a burning animosity toward those whom he feared.

Jenks hated Benko Tatum with an intensity that ate at him like a coyote tearing at a rotting carcass. The bitter venom had seethed within him for years—the old days in the mountains, out in Kansas, and right here and now. But the time was not yet; somehow things were never right. One day Tatum would say the wrong thing and turn away at the wrong time, and Jenks would have his day.

The men broke into the deep snow at the base of the slope and turned toward the rock outcropping where Jasper had disappeared from view.

"I told ya he wasn't dead," Tatum yelled, viciously slapping his horse's neck, as they rounded the point of the hill. "He ain't up there."

Tatum dismounted and scrambled up to the rock ledge where Jasper had landed. "He's got up and headed down the valley," he said, rage filling his rasping voice.

"Whaddaya see?" Teeter hollered.

"Nothin', but 'is hat. He's hurt good, though...bleedin' like a stuck pig," Tatum said, as he disappeared around a rocky bluff.

"If that old coon reaches Fort Bridger, or if his Mormon pals find 'im, our game's up," he hollered back at his two companions.

Jasper's breath was coming in rasping gulps, and he was leaving a distinct trail of blood behind him as he lunged through the deep snow and struggled up the side of a wide, but narrowing gully.

The blizzard had eased in intensity leaving the air frigid and clean, and through the pounding in his ears he could hear Tatum and two of his gang a half mile below, where the gully emptied into the narrow valley. Benko Tatum and his thugs had found his trail, and he could see them, like wolves on the scent of a wounded deer, plowing headlong into the bloody furrow he had left in the deep snow.

Tatum's shot had caught the mountain man low in the back on his right side, and the ugly, ragged wound would not stop bleeding. Staggering through the deep, snow-covered brush, Jasper could feel the warm stickiness spreading beneath his rough wool shirt and down his pant leg. He knew he had to find a place to hide and get the bleeding stopped, but the sloping shoulder of the narrow gully was mostly covered with sage brush and thinly timbered with pinion and juniper. If Tatum or one of his men got sight of him, it all would be over. Jasper knew he was about out of strength—and luck.

Lacking the energy to climb farther, Jasper stumbled at an angle toward the bottom of the snow-smothered gully where the brush appeared to be thicker and offered some concealment. Reaching out to catch himself against an outcropping of rock, his feet, numb from the intense cold and loss of blood, suddenly slipped on the frozen earth beneath the snow and shot out from under him, sending him tumbling headlong into the brush and willows that choked the bottom of the gully.

The pain from the ugly wound was intense, and he fought to hold back a scream. Despite the cold, he felt hot, but his skin was cold and clammy with sweat. Rolling over he looked up into a low, dense roof of willows that under the weight of the deep snow bent in toward a narrow, frozen streambed. He was lying in a small tunnel of white that led downhill toward the base of the gully where it probably joined one of the larger tributaries of the Muddy Fork, maybe even the river itself, in the valley below. Exhausted and weak, he could go no farther, and bunching his shirt in his fist, he pressed it tightly into the wound.

The willows above his head suddenly moved, dusting his hot face with a cold shower of white powder as a strong gust of wind brought a renewal of the blizzard. Jasper slowly sank into the semi-blackness of shock, and the storm began again to build in intensity, drowning out the dimly heard voices of the men on the hillside above him.

Jasper had suspected that Tatum and his gang were camped somewhere between Camp Winfield, the make-shift winter quarters of Alexander's command, and Fort Bridger, controlled by the Mormons. But he had no idea where, and they had caught him flat-footed and vulnerable out in the open.

The snow had not stopped since he and Lot's band had burned the wagon train. It was driven by an intense, frigid wind out of the Northwest, and life was miserable for everyone. Alexander's soldiers were undoubtedly beginning to suffer, their food and other supplies quickly becoming exhausted. And their tents offered slight protection from the bitter cold of the persistent blizzard. Tempers on both sides were short, and real bloodshed was no more than one shot away.

The pain and the intense cold slowly revived him, and the mountain man fought the delirium that insistently pushed at his fevered mind. He could remember the shot. In the cold air it had sounded and felt as if it had come from a cannon, and there was little doubt in his mind from who's deadly Hawken it had come. He was not quite sure what had happened next, but he had been laying face down in the snow some ten feet below a shallow rock ledge, a searing pain in the side of his back that felt as though someone had run him through with a hot poker, the sound of a rifle shot dying among the trees and cliffs of the mountains. He knew he had been shot, and now hearing the distant sound of Tatum's voice and the call of his men, he knew by whom.

Jasper lay still, the cold surrounding him somehow easing the pain. He could hear Tatum and his men making their way up the gully as they struggled to follow his trail; but the blizzard had intensified, and catching a word here and there, he knew they were having a difficult time. His bloody path was quickly disappearing in the storm.

"Ain't no use," the man called Jenks said. "His trail's gone in this snow. We ain't never gonna find 'im in this blizzard, 'an my feet's plumb froze."

Benko Tatum grabbed the man by the arm, swinging him around. "Now...you looky here," he snarled. "He's shot through the lights. I saw it m'self. Teeter knocked 'im plumb off 'is horse and into the canyon, and he ain't slippin' outta this one. You hear me? You ain't near as miserable as he is."

"But...Benko...."

"I got 'im now," Tatum said, pushing past Jenks into the storm. "He's around here somewheres, 'an he's gonna stay got." Surveying what little could be seen of the canyon, he turned to face the two men. We're gonna finish that coon b'fore this day's done," he hissed, wiping the snow from his hairless face. "I don't care if hell freezes over with us."

"Ain't nowhere he coulda crawled off to, Tatum," Teeter said. "Nowhere t' hide but down in them bushes."

Tatum surveyed the hillside, and said, "Reckon so. Let's start pokin' around down there."

Obediah Jones sat watching the blizzard obliterate the world outside his cramped shelter, his eyes watering from the smoke of a small, unenthusiastic fire that belligerently shared the tiny sanctuary. The army scout was tired and his cramped legs ached, but he was comparatively dry and, if not warm, at least not too cold.

He had spent three days scouting the mountains and high prairies around Fort Bridger, and he was sure he would have little to report back to Colonel Alexander that he could not have told him without having to do any scouting in the first place.

The deteriorating weather had caught him in the mountains west of the Muddy Fork, ten or twelve miles northwest of Fort Bridger. He had been working his way toward Echo Canyon, but it had quickly become obvious that the weather was going to get worse before it got better. It was a place where he and Jasper had spent some time years before trapping some of the streams in the area, and he knew it fairly well.

As the clouds had lowered and the wind had picked up, he had led his horse up a familiar narrow canyon and built a lean-to at the mouth of a wide, but shallow, declivity beneath a large, rocky outcropping in the face of the canyon. It was not large or deep enough to be called a cave, but with the lean-to, it made a fairly effective, though cramped, shelter from the storm.

However, too much time in so small a place caused not only physical pain, but mental gloom. And Obediah's mood had lowered with the clouds and thickened with the blowing snow. His only occupation in this damp, tiny place was throwing an occasional stick or twig on the reluctant fire in a half-hearted effort to keep it going. It was as if both man and fire each resented the other's presence as an unwelcome condition of survival.

This is a no win situation. If I ever in my life saw one, this has got to be it, Obediah thought to himself. *Nobody's going to win, everybody's going to get hurt in some way, and here I am right in the middle of it. And Jasper. Now there's something to ponder, Jasper Pughsey running around trying to save the day for the Mormons while I'm doing my best to help that ungrateful Alexander get in a position to do who knows what to those people. Good old Colonel Arrogance himself.*

Obediah picked a stick from a stack of dry branches at his side and poked at the fire with a sullen resentment. *For the life of me, I don't know what this dust-up is all about. The Mormons are out here miles from nowhere trying to establish a life for themselves—and doing a pretty good job of it, too. Back east, the Union's coming apart at the seams—almost war in the Kansas Territory—and the fools send a major army force out here to beat up on a people that hasn't hurt anyone and isn't in a position to cause any trouble if they wanted to—which, as far as I can tell, they don't.*

Sitting up in the cramped space, the mountain man stretched a leg to ease an annoying ache, and the fire seemed to vindictively reach out to sting him.

"Damn," he shouted, but he resentfully resisted kicking the fire out into the storm.

So what if they're dumb enough to want more than one wife. Now, there's one to try and figure out. From all I hear, it's hard enough to get along with just one, but if some of them want more....

An' then Alexander sending me out here to count heads—heads that can't be found when they don't want to be. Mormons! These mountains are crawling with them, but none of them are sticking their heads up just to make my life easier. What does it matter how many of them there are anyway? The sooner Alexander catches on to the fact that it's a different kind of war, the better off we'll all be. There aren't going to be lines of soldiers facing each other. When it starts, these dumb troopers are going to get it from all sides and not know one shot from the other.

"Oh...well," Obediah sighed, attempting to find a more comfortable position while trying to avoid his flickering, ill-tempered companion. Then an even more annoying thought hit him: *As if that isn't enough, add into all of this Benko Tatum and his gang of thugs and you've....*

The thump of a shot from a mountain rifle reverberated up the narrow canyon and invaded his den. It was a sound not easily mistaken—a boom, more than a crack, that carried a sense of finality with it. Adjusting his position so he could poke his head out under the lean-to, Obediah strained to hear what the source of the shot might be.

Leaning back he tried to give the situation some meaning. The last he saw of Jasper Pughsey, the old mountain man was sneaking down on Fort Bridger to steal a horse and warn his Mormon friends. But Benko Tatum and his gang had beaten them to the fort, and Jasper might have had a run-in with them trying to get in.

I should have stayed with him, Obediah thought. *No telling what's happened. That old coot can't get along with himself, let alone anyone else. He probably got down there and wound up in a real fracas. In fact, for all I know, the roof's fallen in and the whole shebang has started.*

The more Obediah thought about the possibilities, the more uncomfortable he became, though it wasn't likely that Alexander would have his troops out in this blizzard. The man was arrogant at times, but he was no fool.

Unfortunately, the same couldn't be said for Benko Tatum.

No, Obediah thought, *this is just the kind of situation a fool like Tatum would try to take advantage of. And this is just the kind of weather Jasper would ignore if he thought there was going to be trouble. And what if he never had a chance to get word of Tatum's scheme to the right people? Or what if he and his raiding pals had gotten caught out in this storm? What would Benko Tatum be up to? For the matter of that, what would Jasper Pughsey be up to?*

Jasper Pughsey lay in his frozen world fighting the unconsciousness that repeatedly swept across him in dark waves. He had lost a great deal of blood, and despite his efforts to stop the bleeding, the wound was large and the bleeding persistent. The ice in the small streambed beneath him was slowly melting into a pink pool that soaked his back, and chills began racking his hot, aching body. The mountain man tried to concentrate on keeping pressure on his painful side, though his shirt had become soaked and his hand sticky with blood.

Through the pain and encroaching delirium, Jasper could hear Benko Tatum somewhere above him prodding the snow-choked bushes that hid the stream. He knew there were others with Tatum and he could hear their urgent shouts growing closer. It was only a matter of time until they found him and put an end to his misery. He almost cried out to hurry the inevitable and the sure relief that would follow.

But something deep inside the old mountain man— some reservoir of will or just plain cussedness—refused the inevitable, refused the pain, refused the delirium, denied him the release of death, from his wound or from the hand of Benko Tatum or one of Tatum's kind. He would not die, he would not go under, not lying here in a miserable puddle of his own making. Nothing was right in this whole thing, not the United States Army about to crush his friends, not Benko Tatum's obsession with destroying him and Obediah Jones. There was no plain dealing or square shooting in any of it, and Jasper Pughsey's will to live rose up out of his pain and out of his delirium and out of the injustice of it all. Right then and there, numb to the bone, and hurting something fierce, he swore he would not go under until it was right.

A stillness fell over the gully as the wind dropped and the snow ceased.

"I tell ya, he's in here somewheres," Tatum hollered to Teeter and Jenks, who were poking the bushes on the other side of the small stream as the three slowly worked their way back down the gully.

"Yeah...an' if we find 'im, he's probably dead," Teeter sneered. "What's the matter with you, anyway, Tatum?"

"Even if 'e ain't dead, he's gonna be anyway," Jenks added. "Besides, I'm near froze."

Tatum slowly straightened up from the willows and brush he had been searching and laid his Hawken at a dangerous angle across his left forearm. "What's the matter with me," he said, in a voice laden with pure poison, "is nobody crosses me an' lives t' tell the story. And Pughsey's time has more'n come fer all a that, and his side kick, too, if I ever draw a bead on him."

The bald trapper eyed the two from beneath the brim of

his hat as they continued their half-hearted search, and his thumb slid slowly up over the hammer of the big rifle. "Truth t' tell," he said slowly, his eyes almost disappearing in a fixed squint of concentration, "I don't know which is more tiresome, Pughsey's slick ways, or your complainin'."

The tone of Tatum's voice caused Teeter to look up and see the big Hawken, not a dozen feet away, pointing in the general direction of his belly. Slowly, he withdrew his rifle from the snow-covered brush, but he knew beyond any shadow of a doubt that if he thumbed the hammer or made any sudden movement, Tatum would strike with little concern for the consequences. He knew Benko Tatum was essentially a loner, and like most of his kind, flocked with others only out of necessity, not from any sense of loyalty or belonging.

Unaware of the mounting tension between his two malevolent cohorts, and concentrating more on his own wretched misery, Jenks continued searching the willows and brush, slowly moving farther down stream. The only thing that offered any relief from the cold was the constant movement that came with prodding the mounds of snow that hid the small streambed. His long rifle poked the snow-covered willows and brush with a slow, thoughtless rhythm that allowed his mind to drift back to the warm hut that awaited the three of them and to forget the constant numbness of his cold, tired feet. The streambed seemed to wander forever downhill, a small bend here and a small turn there, a larger bulge of snow here that required a deeper thrust, and a smaller one there requiring only a slight jab, the weight of the rifle doing most of the work.

He slowly approached a larger mound where some of the snow had fallen through willows and brush and absently shoved the weapon in until his hand was buried in the crusty snow.

Obediah Jones slowly lowered himself into the snow and, cocking his big Hawken, watched from the ridge as Benko Tatum and two of his gang prodded the snow-covered willows and brush below, obviously trying to flush something or someone from hiding. There was no mistaking Tatum, but with their backs to him, the mountain man could not recognize the other two.

From the sign on the other side of the gully, there had been some kind of trouble. They were obviously hunting someone down. Whoever it was had to be seriously hurt, and Obediah had the uncomfortable feeling it was Jasper Pughsey. In fact, something inside told him it was. Anyone else, they would have just left to die from his wounds and the cold. And if it was Jasper they were after, he had to be badly hurt to allow himself to be chased to ground by this scruffy bunch. That would explain the persistence of their search.

From where he lay, the mountain man could hear their voices as the three slowly worked their way down the gully, Tatum facing him on the far side of the streambed and the other two on the near side with their backs to him. But he was too far away to make out what they were saying. Obediah watched with renewed interest as Tatum straightened up and slowly lifted his gun in the direction of the man directly across from him. Judging from the other man's reaction, it was Will Teeter. Something had been said that Tatum didn't like, and the two seemed locked in some sort of stare-down. The tension between them was obviously mounting.

Obediah couldn't help but chuckle. Maybe with any luck at all, Tatum and Teeter would finish one another off, and that would leave him with just the pork eater that was still poking at the bushes and seemed oblivious to everything else. He watched the third man slowly and unheedingly move down stream, away from his two feuding companions.

Halfheartedly, the man shoved his rifle into a new snow mound. Suddenly, in violent reaction, the willows and brush before him unexpectedly exploded in a crystal white cloud that detonated with tremendous force, as if the weapon had burst some frozen container that blew apart from the sudden release of the pressure within it.

Incongruously, the stunned man seemed sucked into the vortex of the convulsion and vanished altogether, as Jasper Pughsey thrust up through the white storm and fired a wild shot in the direction of Benko Tatum and Will Teeter. Then, as suddenly as it had begun, all of its energy expended, the tempest seemed to collapse back into the small streambed, and Jasper Pughsey sank from sight as the white powder slowly settled over the still tormented willows and brush. Stillness settled over the gully as the sound of his unexpected shot reverberated off the sides of the gully and on into the mountains.

Stunned by the suddenness of it all, Tatum and Teeter stood in shocked silence as an almost unnatural calm settled over the frozen, broken river bed.

Tatum could not believe his eyes as he watched the snow settle over the bushes where Jenks and Jasper Pughsey had disappeared.

"Well...I'll be," Teeter stammered. "If that don't beat all. What...."

"Get 'em!" Tatum yelled, forcing his way through the willows and shoving Teeter toward the spot where the two men had disappeared. "Get 'em! We...."

Tatum was cut short in mid-sentence by a heavy boom that seemed to fill the entire gully, and the ball from Obediah Jones' Hawken thudded into the hillside in front of him, sending a stinging spray of snow and ice into his eyes, momentarily blinding him.

"Don't do it, Teeter," someone hollered, as Teeter, searching the hillside above them, started to bring his rifle up. "Not unless you and your bald boss want to end it all. If you want to buy into a final resting place here and now, just try it."

Teeter slowly lowered his rifle as a cursing Benko Tatum rubbed the snow from his sore eyes and focused on one of the two men he hated most in this world. It was Obediah Jones. His frustration was almost more than he could endure. Was there no escape from these two? Was he ever going to get the vengeance he so desperately sought?

"You'll go first, Tatum," Obediah hollered from across the gully, sensing Tatum's pent-up rage.

Obediah Jones stood thirty yards above them beside a large Yellow Pine. He was looking squarely down the barrel of his big Hawken, and there was no question who had the upper hand.

"He's got us," Tatum said, his voice low and filled with anger.

"Benko, you and Teeter, there, had best head on over the hill. And you'd better pray there's nothing permanently wrong with Jasper, or I'll be along right behind you—and you won't like what I bring with me. Now, move it!"

CHAPTER ELEVEN

The President leaned across his large, ornate, dimly lit desk. "Now, let me be sure I understand correctly, Captain Van Vliet. Do you mean to tell me that these people can prevent an army—a rather large army, I might add—from entering the Salt Lake Valley, and that they have threatened to burn their homes if our troops do, in fact, enter their city?"

A dying fire struggled for life across the dark room causing indistinct shadows to rise and fall and seemed to emphasize the cold, late hour.

"Yes sir, that is what I was told...in no uncertain terms," the exhausted officer replied. He stood self-consciously before the big desk, water from his slicker dripping on what was sure to be a very expensive carpet.

The tired, wet soldier had ridden hard for nearly three weeks through the most miserable weather imaginable to make his report as quickly as possible. He had arrived in the dead of night in a cold, driving rain and sleet storm that had turned the streets of Washington into oozing muck.

"By whom? I just don't understand such a thing," the President responded, hotly. "Who told you that?"

"Brigham Young himself, sir."

The President stood up and turned toward the window. "Brigham Young. Brigham Young...King Brigham! That's all I hear. What kind of man is he?" he said, turning to face Van Vliet. "Is he crazy? No man can compel such a thing of the people he governs. Is he a king or something? Is the charge of King Brigham true? Where does the man get such authority?" he demanded.

"Brigham Young is many things, Mr. President." The deep, cultured voice came from the shadows behind the startled Van Vliet. "But the one thing you must understand is that he most assuredly is not crazy. And he is not a king, nor does he consider himself to be such. But as recent events have shown, he is a very effective leader."

"But...no one...I mean...."

"He is determined, sir. And so are his people," the man said, rising from his chair. Moving into the dim light of the desk, he offered his hand to the dripping army officer. "Captain Van Vliet, I'm Thomas Kane."

"I'm sorry, Captain Van Vliet," the President said, apologetically. "This is Colonel Thomas Kane, a friend, and a man with some acquaintance with the Mormons. Some even say he's one of them. Are the rumors true, Thomas?" the President asked, half-jokingly.

"Unfortunately, rumors abound about us all, Mr. President," Kane said, with a wry smile that dismissed the President's intemperate question.

Kane, a short, swarthy man with dark, penetrating eyes, turned from the President and shook the wet soldier's hand vigorously. "Captain, you've obviously had a long, tiring ride. Under adverse circumstances, no doubt."

"I have, sir. I'm afraid I'm in no condition to be standing here ruining this rug."

"Nonsense, Captain. Take off your slicker and sit down. Both of you," the President said, gesturing to four large chairs near the fireplace. "I'll have someone put some life back into those coals," he said, pulling on a sash behind his desk.

"I asked Mr. Kane to be here when I got word of your

arrival. Kane knows these people, worked with them before on a number of occasions. We have been discussing the possibility of his acting as conciliator in this explosive affair."

"Something certainly needs to be done, Mr. President," the exhausted soldier said, taking the chair nearest the fire. "If something isn't done, there could be a great deal of bloodshed." Leaning forward to emphasize his words, he continued, "They will not accept troops into their valley, Mr. President. There's going to be war if something isn't done quickly."

"He is absolutely right, Mr. President," Kane said, waiting for the President to take his chair. "These people have endured far too much in pursuit of their religious beliefs. In my judgment, they are not going to tolerate another Nauvoo."

"Another Nauvoo? What exactly does that mean, Colonel?" the President said, with an obvious lack of patience for argument.

"It simply means that they are not going to be driven again from a city they sacrificed to build in order to worship as they saw fit. That's what happened in Nauvoo, Illinois ten years ago. And several years before that, the Governor of Missouri issued an extermination order against them. They are not going to allow it to happen again, Mr. President. Nor should they have to. And that is precisely how they interpret this whole affair: as one more outrageous attack on their religious beliefs."

"Religious beliefs, indeed," the President huffed. "I tell you, it's a bluff. Nobody is that religious."

"The one thing I can tell you for certain, sir, it's no bluff," Van Vliet said, in a low, tired voice. "I sat in nearly all the meetings of their leaders the few days I was there. I sat in public meetings where almost every man, woman, and child seemed to be in attendance, and there was no disagreement among them—not so much as a murmur."

"Nonsense, Captain," the President said, "that just can't be. I don't see how...."

"Mr. President...in the Sunday meeting I attended—sat on the stand with their leaders, in fact—one of the church Elders, who spoke of the approaching army, as much as asked for a vote from all present—there must have been four thousand or more. When he asked who would apply the torch to their own buildings, cut down their trees, and lay waste to their fields, every hand in the audience shot up at the same moment. I saw not the slightest hint of hesitation," Van Vliet said with emphasis.

"I'm sorry, sir," he continued, "but if you send that army into that valley, assuming they can even get into the Salt Lake Valley, there will be nothing there but smoke and rubble. No houses, no animals, no grain in the fields or barns, and no people. It's just that simple, sir."

"Indeed it is, Mr. President," Kane interjected. "You had better listen to this gentleman. If he has been there, if he has spoken with Brigham Young and the others, if this is what he was told, you can rely on it, sir."

"They can't be serious. They're out on the frontier, they've got nowhere to go, they...."

"Excuse me, sir, but that is exactly the point," Kane responded. "They have nowhere else to go. For the past twenty-five years, they have been driven from pillar to post because of who or what they are. They were driven from state to state and finally from the nation itself, and all because of their religion. In my judgement, they will take it no longer."

"That's right, Mr. President. I don't know when I've seen such determination," said Van Vliet. "If the army had arrived in the mountains even a month earlier, perhaps—just perhaps—they could have forced their way into the valley, but it's too late in the season now. If we persist, those troops are either going to run straight into a bloody rock wall, or into a deserted, desolate desert valley—if they don't freeze first."

The room fell silent as a servant entered the room with an arm full of wood. As he laid the logs, the fire responded hungrily, and the shadows became more lively.

"That'll be fine, Isaiah. Leave us now, please."

The door closed silently, and Thomas Kane said, "Assuming they can get into the Salt Lake Valley, Mr. President, there will be nothing there for your officials to govern. Nothing at all."

The President rose from the fire and returned to his desk. The big chair squeaked in complaint as the fifteenth President of the United States leaned back and looked at the ceiling, lost in thought. Finally, he heaved a great sigh and leaned forward, his gaze shifting between Van Vliet and Kane.

"Gentlemen, what more am I to do? In all of my experience in government, I have never seen such an uproar," he said, thumping his desk with the flat of his hand. "Everyone—and I mean everyone—is calling for the Mormon ulcer to be cut out. They are universally seen as outlaws, gentlemen—outlaws!"

The President pushed his chair back and returned to his place by the fire. "Why, even Douglas—Stephen A. Douglas, of all people—is after them, and I mean he's after them. Why, the fool has even called for repeal of the act creating the Utah Territory," he said, his fist hitting the arm of his chair for emphasis. "The man has waxed so passionate, he seems to have forgotten that he's the author of the Utah Organic Act."

The President stood and began pacing the floor. "It would seem that his great principle of popular sovereignty applies only to those he sees fit to bestow it on," the President said, his distaste for Douglas apparent in his sarcasm. "Well, the Republicans are not letting him get away with it. That much I can tell you, gentlemen," he said, his arm waving in the direction of his two visitors. "They've been all over him for his absurd position. All he has done is protect Brigham Young and his crew. The Mormons have simply applied the Douglas doctrine of self-government to suit their own needs, that's all."

"That's true, Mr. President," Colonel Kane said, interrupting the President's bitter outburst. "Everything they have done, they have done lawfully in establishing their western colonies."

"Well...be that as it may, gentlemen," the President said, returning to his chair, "things have simply gone too far. They are out of my hands; I can do nothing. Colonel Cook left Fort Leavenworth with Governor Alfred Cumming weeks ago, and Colonel Johnston and his staff left to assume command at about the same time. They have all probably reached Alexander's headquarters by now," the President said, sitting forward, his head cocked oddly to one side.

Though few people realized it, the President had an eye defect that was a constant irritation to him. But in compensating for it, he gave the appearance of great courtesy in conversation, regardless of the emotion of the moment.

"I tell you things have simply gone too far. They are out of my hands; I can do nothing." With a sigh that seemed filled with despair, the President leaned back in his chair and stared into the fire.

After a long silence, punctuated by the crackling, incongruously cherry fire, Thomas Kane, his voice low, said, "You must do something to put an end to it, Mr. President. Things, cannot be allowed...."

"But how, man?" the President broke in. "I'm being made to look like a fool now as it is. Those idiots in Congress are at me like hounds to the fox. They're claiming that I've botched the whole thing, that I've mismanaged the invasion," the President said, leaving his chair and again pacing the floor of his office. "To back out now...to recall Cumming and Johnston after all of this...."

"Mr. President," Kane began, "you're facing certain political disaster unless you...."

"Don't speak to me of disaster, man," the President responded. "I am daily in the midst of disaster. And to make matters worse, this all has to be out west. It's just more sectionalism...it's just another powder keg among many that threatens to blow us apart."

The President returned to his chair at the fire, his voice more calm. "I'm sorry gentlemen, but if I back down now, how can I hold this nation together, with the conflict over Kansas and the South almost in open rebellion? When the Senate is in session, it's heard every day."

"There is no question that things are serious, Mr. President, but...."

"Serious, Mr. Kane?" the President responded. "You speak of political disaster. I tell you, sir, we are on the verge of total civil war, and there is precious little I can do about it. This nation is about to slide apart section by section, state by state almost, and this Brigham Young fellow is just like all the rest. If he can't have it his way, then the answer is resistance to the laws of these United States."

"But that is just the point, Mr. President. He is not a secessionist. Neither he nor his people see themselves as being apart from the United States," Kane said, sitting forward to emphasize his argument. "To the contrary, sir, they want to be left alone in peace, and they see in the Constitution and its guarantees of religious liberty their only safety. Not only do they not want separation, it is my firm belief they would like nothing better than statehood, if they were guaranteed all of the equalities of citizenship. They have tried in the past, as you well know."

"Then why will he not obey the law and receive our army? Tell me that, sir. Why are they attacking our troops and supplies in the dead of winter, burning our soldier's supplies? Answer me that, sir. I tell you, I fear for Cumming's life."

"Mr. President, I am no statesman," Captain Van Vliet said, leaning forward in his chair. "I'm just a soldier, and a Quartermaster at that. But just days ago, I sat in Mormon meetings; I talked with Brigham Young and others, and these are not a people caught up in insurrection. They are not rebelling against the United States and declaring independence. They are reacting to the presence of a hostile army approaching their city. They are simply trying to defend themselves from what they see as another invading force. And if we persist, sir, it is their plan of operation to defend themselves by burning the grass, cutting up the roads, and stampeding the animals until the snow falls."

"It falls early in that country, Mr. President," Colonel

Kane interjected.

"Indeed it does," Van Vliet said. "In fact, the night before I left Fort Bridger, snow fell in the mountains. It won't be long, sir, before the canyon passes are choked with snow and the roads impassable."

"To them, Mr. President, it is just more religious persecution," Kane said. "Let me emphasize, sir, that it was merely a decade ago that they were driven from their homes at Nauvoo, Illinois, the largest city in Illinois, I might add—a city they built. They were slaughtered, pillaged, their women raped, and finally driven across the Mississippi in the dead of winter. They sought safety out west, not secession."

The President sighed and, returning to his chair, stared into the fire, a sense of melancholy subduing his belligerence. Neither of his companions felt the need to break the silence, which was punctuated only by the sound of two well-burned logs collapsing in the dying fire, sending a spiral of bright sparks up the chimney. Finally, the President drew a deep breath, and said, "That fire needs another log."

"Perhaps there is an answer, Mr. President," Thomas Kane said, breaking the moody atmosphere that had descended on the room. "I know you are somewhat reluctant, but as we have discussed, let me go out to Salt Lake Valley and talk with Young. Let me go as your emissary, your conciliator, and see if I can bring this unfortunate incident to a close before tragedy overtakes us."

"I'm tired, Mr. Kane," the President said, pulling himself erect in his chair. "At least you propose a solution. That is more than most are doing these days."

"Thank you, Mr President," Thomas Kane said, rising

from his chair. "I take that as my commission, and I will be on my way within the next few days. As soon as I can finalize arrangements."

"You may use my name, Thomas, but you do it of your own volition. You have my blessing, but I can send you with precious little more."

"I understand, sir. I know how tired you must be. It is time that Captain Van Vliet and I are on our way. We have more to discuss, but we needn't take more of your time."

The President of the United States rose from his chair and briefly shook each man's hand, his grip tenuous and unsure. "Thank you, gentlemen," he said, following Kane and Van Vliet to the door where all three paused.

"Maybe Stanton was right," the President said, his voice heavy with discouragement and the late hour.

"How's that, Mr. President?" Kane asked, somewhat subdued by the President's mood.

"He told me, not too long ago, that I was sleeping on a volcano, that the ground under me was mined all around and ready to explode. He said that if I did not act soon and with promptness, I might be the last President of the United States. What do you think, Thomas?"

"What do I think, Mr. President?" Kane asked, taking a slow breath. "I think these are undoubtedly perilous times; I think these United State have never been more threatened by events born of history and borne of misunderstanding; I think we are at some sort of crossroad, the nature of which no one really understands—not Stanton, not Douglas, and certainly not me."

Kane took the President's hand in a strong, reassuring grip.

"But of this I feel sure," he said, looking hard at the

defeated man before him, "no nation in history has had a more sure foundation than ours. If we can surmount this moment in history, if we can work out our differences in a Christian, decent manner, we have the capacity to come out of these conflicts the strongest nation the world has ever known."

"But can I...?"

"You can, sir. You must."

"But I have so little with which to do it, man," the President said, opening the heavy door.

Thomas Kane paused in the hallway, and in an effort at reassurance said, "I know Brigham Young and his people, Mr. President. They will do what they consider to be right, and you needn't fear for Governor Cumming. He will be safe enough, but your army is another thing altogether."

"Thomas, I will look forward to your report, and I pray for your success. You're right, you know, this nation does stand at the crossroads. I fear for her future."

The two men stood under the portico watching the heavy downpour as a black carriage drawn by two equally black horses drew up in front of them.

A liveryman opened the dripping door, and Kane said, "Let me drop you at your quarters, Captain."

Settling back in the comfortable leather seat, Van Vliet asked, "Can he do it, Colonel Kane? Are we going to be successful in saving this Union?"

"About the South...about slavery, I am not the one to say, Captain," Kane said, attempting to be heard over the sound of the heavy rain. "But as for the Mormon problem, there remains much goodwill under all of the intolerance—

at least on their part. Brigham Young will do what is right, whether he is backed into a corner by his government or not."

"But the President seems so...."

"Don't underestimate the man, Captain Van Vliet. He is a man of vast experience. He was President Polk's Secretary of State, as you undoubtedly know, and he has been ambassador to two different countries. But more importantly, on top of it all, he is a gentleman, a man essentially of goodwill. Yes, he feels inadequate, old perhaps, overwhelmed by events. But, though I don't necessarily agree with his view of his powers, I'm not so sure that if I were in his shoes right now, I wouldn't feel much the same. Would you?"

Colonel Albert Sidney Johnston handed the letter he had been reading to the portly, round-faced gentleman sitting across the small table from him. "Here's Alexander's communiqué," he said, in a subdued tone. "I'm afraid it is not at all reassuring."

"And why is that, suh?" Governor Alfred Cumming asked, his words laden with a heavy Georgian accent.

"Even with Phelps' and Reno's batteries there for a week or more, Alexander's force seems to have been brought to a standstill by the Mormons, many of their supplies burned, and the weather turning against them," Johnston replied.

Retrieving the letter from the table top, Colonel Johnston said, "Listen to this, Governor. 'The Mormons are committing acts of hostility and depredation, and have already burnt three trains containing supplies.'"

"'The season is late and the time in which military

operations can be affected is very limited; the total supply of forage will last only fourteen days, and it is evident that before the expiration of that time the troops must either be at their wintering place, or from loss of animals they will be unable to transport supplies to it.'"

"Let me see the lettah, Colonel," the Governor said, reaching across the table. "He's moah than right about the season. The days are gettin' shortah and coldah, and these old Georgia bones about froze last night. Let me see, now," he said, adjusting his reading spectacles.

The tent fell quiet as the Governor studied Alexander's report. The only noise to be heard was the occasional turning of a page and the energetic sound of troopers busy breaking camp in preparation for the coming day's march.

At length, the Governor cleared his throat, and said, "Well, foah a man who does not know fully the intentions of his gove'nment, he has so fah done the correct thing. Wouldn't you say so, Colonel?"

"Yes, I would," Johnston said, rising from the table. "Alexander's a competent officer, though I do think his plans to move to Fort Hall for the winter are more ambitious than the lateness of the season will allow—judging, at least, from the way things feel around here."

Governor Cumming responded with a grunt as he pushed himself up from the table and followed the Colonel out into the busy camp site.

No sooner had the two men stepped outside, than a half dozen troopers, under the direction of their Sergeant, swarmed around the tent, emptying its contents and bringing it down for folding and storage aboard one of the wagons.

As Johnston walked with Cumming to the Governor's

waiting carriage, officers and Sergeants could be heard shouting orders, and the chaos of the disintegrating camp soon took on the order of an army ready for movement.

"I feel disaster in my bones, Governor," the Colonel said, taking the reins of his horse from a Corporal and swinging easily into the saddle. "This expedition is on the very edge of disaster. If the Mormons don't put an end to it first, the weather is likely to."

Brigham Young had read Colonel Alexander's letter of October 12th a dozen times or more, and now he sat slumped at his desk listening to General Daniel Wells read it aloud to the assembled brethren. Each time the Prophet had read it, he could not believe that things had come to so tragic an impasse.

From where he sat, the Prophet watched the traffic moving along muddy South Temple Street in the cold morning drizzle. It had rained most of the night, and the coming day offered little promise. The clouds were low and thick, and the morning was dark. A day to match the mood, the Prophet thought to himself. His chair squeaked, much to his annoyance, as he turned to concentrate on Wells' words.

No one stirred as each man in the room listened intently to the army commander's response to their leader's proclamation, and the Prophet studied their faces—the faces of men in whom he had placed so much confidence and trust over the long and difficult years. It required little effort to discern their reactions. Like himself, every man present felt the weight of the burden being imposed upon them by the very government that constitutionally owed them its protection, but that in the past had offered so little in the face of vicious persecution.

Daniel Wells glanced up as he cleared his throat, and then continued, "'You have resorted to open hostilities, and of a kind, permit me to say, very far beneath the usages of civilized warfare, and only resorted to by those who are conscious of an inability to resist by more than honorable means, by authori....'"

A loud murmur of disbelief filled the room, and several voices spoke out in angry denial that such a libelous and outright insulting charge could be made against them and their Prophet. And the despondency of spirit that had marked the meeting quickly burst into anger.

"Has any blood been shed?" the Prophet asked quietly, his voice quickly restoring calm.

"Strict orders were given, President Young, just as you requested," General Wells responded. "And I am certain that with all of the energy our men have visited upon the enemy, not one life has been lost. In fact to my knowledge, no bone has been broken."

"What, in fact, have our men done, Daniel?"

"Under the leadership of men such as Lot Smith and Porter Rockwell, and with the invaluable help of Jasper Pughsey, our men have made their presence known throughout the mountains between here and South Pass. We have engaged the enemy by raiding and burning their supply wagons and in stampeding their horses and cattle. Such had to be done to convince the enemy of our serious determination to keep their force from entering the Salt Lake Valley, and for no other reason. If shots have been fired, Brother Brigham, they have been warning shots or shots to stampede cattle. To my knowledge, none of our men have fired in anger, despite the provocation. Our enemies have undoubtedly lost a great deal of pride, but no loss of life."

"And how much damage has been done?" the Prophet asked.

"To the best of my knowledge, as of October 5th, some seventy-four freight wagons have been destroyed and their contents either confiscated or burned with the wagons. By now there has been a good deal more damage, I'm sure."

"Will that prevent them from entering our valley?"

General Wells turned to the man sitting to the right of President Young, and said, "It hurts them, President Kimball. These wagons have been full to the brim with food, tents, ammunition, and other provisions. But that's not the full story."

"Well...what is the rest?"

"They have lost much of their cattle and many horses. In addition, the weather is our greatest ally. The mountains are already accumulating snow, and I don't think it will be long before Colonel Alexander is forced to find winter quarters for his army."

"Which means?" President Kimball asked.

"Which means, Heber, that we have effectively stopped them—at least for the winter."

"But still he threatens us," the Prophet sighed.

"He does."

"Read it, Daniel."

General Wells shuffled the pages of the long letter and cleared his throat. "Quote: 'It is my duty to inform you that I shall use the force under my control, and all honorable means in my power to obey literally and strictly the orders under which I am acting. If you, or any acting under your orders, oppose me, I will use force, and I warn you that the blood that is shed in this contest will be upon your head. My means I consider ample to overcome any obstacle; and I assure you that any idea you may have formed of forcing these troops back, or of preventing them from carrying out the views of the government, will result in unnecessary violence and utter failure.'"

General Wells laid the letter on President Young's desk and took his seat. Aside from the occasional squeak of a chair, the room fell silent.

At length, the Mormon leader stood and walked to the window. The day had grown darker with the mood of the men in his office, and the street outside had become a sea of mud, making it seem to those caught in the persistent downfall that no progress could be made—none at all.

CHAPTER TWELVE

"No, sir...not hide ner hair of 'im," Sergeant O'Riley said, standing at attention before his commanding officer's campaign desk. "Not in a week'r more, now, sir."

Colonel Alexander rose from the small desk and walked around the big Irishman to the tent flap and peered out into the snow storm.

"Well...I'd like—I need—a disposition report from Jones before I attempt any movement. I've got to do something soon. I had no idea he'd be gone this long."

"Beggin' the Colonel's pardon, sir, but countin' Mormon noses in this blasted, God-forsaken country, if I do say so meself, sir—meanin' no disrespect, sir—ain't a sure-fire thing, what with the weather an' all...."

"Stand at ease, Sergeant," Alexander said, returning to his cramped desk and slumping down into a moody silence.

Somehow, Alexander seemed to feel that he always thought better with his Top Sergeant near at hand, and he frequently fell into silent contemplation when faced with a particularly knotty problem, leaving the big Irishman standing awkwardly before him not knowing exactly what to say or do. It was happening more and more frequently and caused the big Sergeant a mildly annoying discomfort he could never seem to find the means to avoid.

"Beggin' yer...."

"What you say is true enough," Alexander said, stirring from his thoughts, "but I've got to make some decisions—with or without Jones. Staying here for the winter is a poor option—no option at all, in fact. It's increasingly obvious we

191

either need to get into the Great Salt Lake Basin or find more suitable winter quarters. There's no forage here, and little of the kind of shelter the men need."

"It is, indeed, sir. There's a lot of grumblin, and the deeper the snow gets, the more bored the men are becomin'. The usual chores ain't enough, sir."

"Sergeant, tell the Executive Officer to get in here with any maps we have of the area between here and Great Salt Lake City," the Colonel said, with an air of authority that signaled a decision had been made. "And get my senior officers here, too. Staff meeting in thirty minutes."

Within ten minutes, the command tent was crowded with officers from Alexander's Tenth Infantry, the Fifth Infantry, and Captains Phelps' and Reno's Batteries, each of which had arrived at Camp Winfield a few days earlier.

"Gentlemen, you can easily see that the conditions here are becoming deplorable," Colonel Alexander said, thumping his small map table, "and it takes little imagination to see what the future holds if we stay here much longer. The season is late, and the time in which military operations can be affected with any efficiency at all is very limited, if not gone altogether."

Looking through the small group of officers crowded around the small map table, Alexander saw O'Riley standing near the tent flap. "Sergeant O'Riley, what is the status of our supplies."

"Well, sir," O'Riley said, clearing his throat and rising to his full stature. "That is to say, sir...not so good. With much luck, as you know sir, seven ox trains got through a couple of days ago with provisions that might last as long as five months, dependin' on the severity of the weather, but there's no forage for the animals—and that's our biggest problem."

"How much forage, Sergeant?" Alexander asked.

"Maybe two weeks. Three at the outside, sir."

"Well, there you have it, gentlemen. We seem to be hemmed in by a more than determined enemy in a severe land, and the weather is deteriorating and promising cruel punishment for men and animals alike. The Mormons are committing acts of hostility and depredation almost daily and have only recently burned three trains containing desperately needed supplies. Those that did arrive safely did so only under heavy military guard."

Looking around at the other officers, Captain Jesse Reno asked, "Well...what are our options, Colonel Alexander?"

"Precious few, Captain. We can't fight the Mormons, because we can't find them, and assaulting Fort Bridger would not only be bloody for all, it is beyond my orders. And, in any event, I wouldn't think of such a thing before Colonel Johnston arrives to take command. Secondly, we could wait out the winter right here, but morale would quickly deteriorate and we have only enough forage for three weeks at the outside, leaving us with the unpleasant option of watching all of our animals starve. And that, gentlemen, brings me to the object of this meeting."

One of the company officers, Captain Jesse A. Gove, raised a hand for recognition, and asked, "May I say something, Colonel?"

"You may, Captain Gove. I understand you've been saying a great deal in any event."

"I'm sorry sir, but many of the company and junior officers, myself included, have resented a certain lack of consultation on your part, and can't understand our failure," Gove said, emphasizing the word, "to push on toward Salt Lake City. Rumors have spread that we may even be going back. Quite frankly, sir, we are all being made to look like fools."

"Captain Gove, I am well aware of the criticisms you and others have been making, and I frankly find them offensive, unmilitary, and uncalled for," Alexander said, thumping his desk. "Let not one of you forget that I am the senior officer present. Furthermore, let me remind you all, I have received no information on the position or intentions of the new commanding officer, and I probably won't until—if and when—he finally arrives. And unless you all," he said, waving his hand toward Gove and the other officers, his anger rising, "have received orders or wisdom of which I am unaware, we all remain in utter ignorance of the objects of the government in sending us out here in the first place." The Colonel stared in silence at his officers and then slammed his fist on the table, causing several objects to spill to the floor. "Nor, as you are all aware, have I received any instructions as to what our conduct is to be now that we are out in this God-forsaken place."

Each officer in the tent searched for a spot on the table or tent wall at which he could stare to avoid meeting his commanding officer's angry eyes.

Looking directly at Gove, Alexander continued, "Furthermore, gentlemen, I will brook no further criticism of my actions. As senior officer, I have taken command, and I will have the Executive Officer place under arrest the next man who breaks military discipline. If you have questions or complaints, please have the courtesy to bring them directly to me."

Captain John Phelps was the first to break the embarrassing silence that followed Alexander's sharp rebuke. "Sir?"

"Captain Phelps."

"Let me say, sir, that under the circumstances, you have conducted this difficult operation admirably. While I share the frustrations felt by everyone—speaking for myself—I think there will be no more criticisms from those upon whom you must rely and should be able to trust." Looking at those around him, he continued, "Every man here is more than aware that the fanaticism we have faced has been equal to military organization and discipline. Under the circumstances, I think your command of this miserable situation has been more than admirable."

Murmurs of agreement filled the tent.

"Thank you, Captain".

"I apologize, sir," Gove said curtly.

"Given the difficulties of our situation, what I have taken as past offenses are forgotten," Alexander said, with a tone intended to set the men more at ease. "Now, gentlemen to the purpose of the meeting. I have decided upon the following points: first, the need for a speedy move to more suitable winter quarters; second, the selection of a point of wintering; and third, the best method of conducting the troops and supplies to the point selected."

The reaction among the officers at this unexpected news broke the tension that had filled the tent. Each had fully expected the command to remain at Camp Winfield until the weather broke or until spring.

"As to the first point," Alexander said, clearing his throat to regain attention. "I recently received intelligence that Colonel Johnston will not arrive before the end of the month, the 20th of October at the earliest. That being the case, I have decided to move."

With the prospect of some kind of action, the tent filled the buzz of approval, with the exception of Reno, who said, "If I may, Colonel. I have only just arrived, but I can tell you that with the amount of moisture in the ground and with the snow starting to accumulate, the movement of batteries and wagons may prove a fatal mistake, sir."

"I'd be less than honest if I didn't voice the same fears, Colonel," Phelps said.

"I understand what the two of you are saying, Captain Phelps. I, too, would be less than honest if I didn't say that I share your concerns. But the fact is, gentlemen, we are faced with few options—all of them almost equally depressing. Of course, our first option is to stay put, but with our forage nearly depleted, that option would be totally destructive of our orders."

Alexander's finger went to a point at the right side of the map. "But there are others, the first being to turn back to South Pass and winter over here on the east side of the Wind River mountains."

"But what would that buy us, Colonel?" someone asked.

"Nothing, so far as I can tell, except extra effort and lost time in the spring. It would constitute a one hundred and ten mile retreat, and we would still face a harsh winter there."

"And the Mormons," one of the officers observed, "could well conclude that they had driven us out of their territory and won."

Ignoring the comment, Alexander slid his finger at an angle down the map to a point south of their present position. "Our second option would be to move to Henry's Fork of the Green River to a place appropriately called Brown's Hole."

"That seems a better option," Phelps said.

"Well...not really," the Colonel said, with a sigh born of exhaustion and frustration. "I'm told by Mr. Jones, our scout, that it is a valley on the Green River about ninety miles south of us that is completely encircled by mountains and that it offers good feed for our stock."

"But the biggest problem is, sir...." O'Riley began to offer.

"Yes...our biggest problem is that it is inaccessible to our supply wagons. Thank you, Sergeant."

"And, if I might add, sir," O'Riley interjected, "them blasted Mormons would probably burn the grass first chance they got, sir."

"Well said, Sergeant. Well said. The ever-present Mormons."

"And the third?" someone asked, with an obviously discouraged tone of voice.

"Somewhere in the vicinity of Fort Hall on Beaver Head mountain," Alexander said, tapping a point near the top of the map. "There's an old trading post there that was established some twenty or so years ago, and it still serves as a way station on the Oregon Trail."

"Any drawbacks there, Colonel?," one of the officers asked.

"Without question," Alexander said, sliding the large map to the floor and replacing it with a smaller, more detailed chart, "but that is the option I have chosen, gentlemen."

Pointing to the new map, the Colonel said, "From here, it is a trek of one hundred and forty miles. We'll go by the following route: up Ham's Fork, on which we are now camped, about eighteen miles, to the road called Sublette's

Cutoff," he said, tapping a spot on the map with his finger. "This is a short-cut from Green River to Bear River, and we'll avoid the much longer route by way of Fort Bridger. Furthermore, we might be able to elude some of our Mormon friends by going this way." Tracing the map with his finger, he continued, "Taking Sublette's Cut-off, we will proceed to Bear River and Soda Spring, and then by the emigrant road to the north east, where I am assured good wintering valleys can easily be found. I am further assured that at Fort Hall there are ample herds of cattle which should provide food enough."

Alexander straightened up from the table, looked at his officers, and said, "Any questions?" His tone of voice was that of a man who had made a difficult decision and would brook no argument.

"There being none, we will break camp at first light the day after tomorrow. Will that give sufficient time Sergeant O'Riley?

"Indeed it will, sir. I'll see to it."

"One final thought, then. Prior to leaving on a scouting trip, Mr. Jones indicated that if the Mormons react to our movement at all, they are likely to make a stand at a fortified place near Soda Spring. If this happens, we cannot submit to defeat. In fact, whether we are attacked or not, I have determined that we are going to force our way into the valley of the Bear River and occupy some of the Mormon Villages."

With the unexpected news that at last, they might be allowed to fight, Alexander's officers erupted in a loud chorus of approval. At last they would be given the opportunity to bring force against their elusive enemies.

Captain Jesse Gove's voice was heard above the others.

"Colonel, this is all most of us have been waiting for. If we can just be allowed to retaliate against the depredations these Mormons have been heaping upon us, I can assure you the men will be behind you one hundred percent, sir."

"Mr. Gove, let me remind you that in this army, the men will be one hundred percent behind their officers regardless. Is that understood, sir?" Alexander's meaning and implied threat was apparent to all and quickly restored silence to the tent.

"Indeed, it is, sir, but...."

"It is my feeling, gentlemen," Alexander said, ignoring Gove's attempt at further explanation, "that after such a defeat, the Mormons will be willing to cooperate with us. If we can get possession of a town in the Bear River valley, we can easily fortify and hold it all winter. Gentlemen," Alexander concluded, "I see in this march, not only a sound strategy, but the tactics to bring the Mormons to heel. If we are successful in this march, Brigham Young will have little alternative but to allow us to enter the Territory of Utah and Salt Lake City."

A heavy vapor of damp, gray fog crept slowly through the dense pine forest like a thick cloud of slowly swarming locusts, finding its way around and through each tree, smothering everything in its path. Nothing escaped, and it enveloped Jasper Pughsey with a chilling weight that almost seemed to crush him and caused trickles of cold perspiration to course down his aching body like columns of fire ants. His heart contracted with a kind of irrational fear, and he wanted desperately to scratch his prickling skin.

He knew he had to do something, but the fog was so

heavy with cold and dampness that it was difficult to move, and for some unexplainable reason his feet seemed glued to the crawling forest floor; it took all of the strength he had just to shuffle one foot in front of the other. Each struggling step seemed more difficult, and he knew that they were catching up, that they would find him despite the fog, that somehow they were able to move faster than he, unhampered by the swirling mists, by the fire ants, by heavy, heavy feet. He fought to scratch the ants and to struggle away from his pursuers; but they were close now, and he could hear his name.

"Jasper."

The whole world seemed to shake, and it was hot and heavy.

"Jasper! Come out of it, man."

The fog suddenly vanished, and Jasper looked up into the concerned face of the one man he could count on under any circumstance—Obediah Jones.

"Hold still, Jasper. You've been hurt bad," Obediah said, holding Jasper down as he struggled out of his delirium. "You'll tear that wound open again," he warned.

"Get this thing offa me," Jasper demanded, shoving the heavy buffalo blanket aside. "I'm near drowned in m' own sweat."

"You were hit hard, old timer, and you've had a fever that I thought was going to burn you up for sure," Obediah said, straightening up and walking across the room to a pot-bellied stove. Returning, he thrust a steaming, fragrant mug of hot broth under Jasper's nose. "Drink this. You haven't had anything to eat in a couple of days, and I need to get some strength into you."

Jasper took the hot mug in his cold hands and savored

the pungent aroma of the golden liquid.

"Durned if that don't smell like pure ambrosia," Jasper said, exhaustion making his voice heavy. "What is it?" he asked, taking a slow, loud, hesitant sip.

"I killed a sage hen and made some soup."

"I swear I ain't had nothin' thet tasted so good in a coon's age," the mountain man said, taking a more generous gulp.

"Well...I'm glad, partner, because you need it in the worst way."

Jasper grunted agreement. "Where are we?" he asked, looking up through what remained of a badly burned roof into the dark, grey sky.

"We're in what's left of Fort Bridger.

"Fort Bridger?" Jasper said, choking on a mouthful of soup. "The Mormons burned it about a week ago."

"Burned it? What fer? How long have I been out, anyway, Obediah? What's happenin'?" Jasper asked, struggling once again to get out of his make-shift bed.

"Now...sit down, Jasper," Obediah said, as he gently eased the dizzy Jasper Pughsey back into his place. "You open that wound again, and I'll be planting you out yonder."

"Yeah," Jasper said, what little color he had draining from his drawn face. "I reckon ma'be you're right."

"Maybe, nothing. Here drink more of this, and we'll talk."

As Obediah described the past two days, it all came back to Jasper. His last truly conscious thought was in the ice tunnel at the bottom of the gully, with the sound of Benko Tatum's voice growing nearer.

"...and on top of that, I've had to drag you around these mountains to try and find a place to hole up until you can get your strength back. I was hoping the Mormons would be able to care for you, so I could get back to Alexander's camp and try to keep the lid on things; but when we got here, this was all there was," Obediah said, glancing around the cluttered remains of the room.

"Obediah...we got problems."

"You're telling me?"

"I tell ya," Jasper said, responding a little too energetically and wincing at the pain in his side, "Tatum and them coons what faller him around's gonna start somethin' purty serious if we don't put a stop t' it."

"Well, your right about one thing, they're up to no good and have got to be stopped, but you're not going anywhere soon."

"Whaddaya mean. We gotta...."

"We gotta, nothing," Obediah said, heatedly. "It took me two hours to get you sewed up and the bleeding stopped. You haven't got enough blood left in you to leave a trail from here to the nearest tree. Open that wound again, and Tatum has won. It's as simple as that."

"Well...damn and tarnation, if thet don't beat all," the mountain man said slumping back with weakness and frustration.

Obediah looked down at his old partner. "You going to be all right, Jasper?"

"What're ya askin' a dern fool thing like thet fer? Ya can plainly see I ain't goin' under no time soon."

"I can't plainly see any such thing," Obediah said, struggling into his large buffalo skin coat. "You look more dead than alive right now."

"Where you goin'?"

"I've got to get back to Alexander's camp and let them

know what's happened here. Stay put, and I'll be back in a couple of days. Alexander's as antsy as a horse at the sound of a rattle, and I've got to get back and let him know what's happened."

"Well, now...ain't I showed 'im he's got good reason t' be antsy?" Jasper asked, a wide grin splitting his face.

"More than once, you ornery old coon. The trouble is, he doesn't take too kindly to you and your Mormon friends making off with his supplies."

"Well, them pony soldiers ain't got no business...."

"Maybe so, but they're here, and they're under orders. And the one thing I know about Alexander is that he'll do what's expected of him, regardless of the cost. He's not the easiest man to work with, but he's a mighty fine soldier, Jasper. Best you respect him."

"Ain't none of us what started this fracas, Obediah. This whole thing'll stop soon as he does."

"All it's going to take, Jasper, is one shot. And it won't matter if it's in anger or an accident. One shot, and this entire powder keg'll blow sky high."

"And jest who d' yew think's gonna fire thet shot."

"Well...old timer," Obediah said, stopping at the door. "I've got a hunch you know that as well as I do. For all either of us knows that first shot's been fired, and it took you down."

"Damnation!"

"Yeah. Just you lie there and think on that for a while." Turning back to the door he said, "Don't you get out of that bed except for more soup. It's on what's left of the stove."

"Now...yew wait jest a minute. Yew...."

"If I'm not back in a couple of days, I probably won't be coming back."

* * *

The door to the hut opened and a cold blast whipped the fire wildly, blowing hot ashes out of the fireplace and scattering them around Benko Tatum's feet. Stirring from his reverie, he turned and hollered, "Shut that da...."

"Somethin's up, Tatum," Will Teeter said, slamming the door and slapping the snow and cold from his coat.

Tatum slumped back in his chair and moodily stared into the newly excited fire. "Ain't nothin' up in this weather," he responded irritably. "Put some more wood on this here fire, and do it now before it dies again."

Grabbing a couple of split logs from a careless stack near the door, Teeter walked to the fire and heedlessly threw them into the flames. "I tell ya, somethin's up in that army camp, Benko. Things's startin' t' move down there."

"What're ya talkin' about?"

"Looks t' me like their fixin' to move."

"Move?" Tatum said, sitting up in his chair. "What d'ya mean, move?"

"I mean...I sat an' watched fer the better part of a' hour, till I thought either me or the horse was gonna freeze, and them troops is making all the sign of breaking camp," Teeter said, removing his coat and taking a seat near the fire. "Permanent like."

"You gotta be plum loco. It's gotta be near zero out there. Who'd be crazy enough to do a fool thing like that?"

"I tell ya, it's so, Benko," Teeter said, holding the palms of his hands to the fire. "Loco'r not, they're gonna be on the move—and soon."

Benko Tatum leaned forward and stared moodily into the flames, his mind exploring the possibilities.

"Benko, it looks t' me like now's...."

"Hesh up...I'm thinkin'."

Knowing Tatum's likely reaction to any further suggestions, Teeter got up and walked to the small window overlooking the down-hill slope that fell sharply away from the hut's front wall. The snow was not deep, and in places the frozen ground was bare, but a bitterly cold wind was blowing out of the northwest that seemed to hold the promise of snow. The sky was gray, but the clouds had not yet started to lower.

Tatum spoke so softly that Teeter at first did not hear him clearly. Turning, Teeter said, "Did you say somethin', Benko?"

Tatum turned and snarled, "What I said was, if we was t' figger out where they was headin', an' if we was to get out a head of 'em, we could put a few hot balls int' their sides. An', unless I miss my guess, all creation'd likely blow apart. Them Mormons and them pony soldiers'd be shootin' each other on sight."

"Yer right, Benko," Teeter said, with a chuckle. "An' guess who'd get his whiskers hung out t' dry fer startin' the whole shebang?"

"That's right, and by both sides. That coon Pughsey couldn't dig a whole deep enough t' hide in. Everybody'd be huntin' his scalp."

"Looks t' me like this is exactly what you've been waitin' fer Benko. I gotta hand it to ya."

"Roust them good fer nothin's out," Benko said, pointing to the low loft at the other end of the small room. "Time's here t' start movin'."

"Only one left is Jenks, Benko."

Tatum whirled around from the fire. "Jenks? Where's them other...."

"Jenks said they took off—jest like all the others done."

"They said they was sick of it all, Benko," Jenks said, as he climbed down from the low loft. "What with the cold, an' all, they was...."

"Then the three of us is gonna do it. Like I said, time's here t' start movin'. Them others made the wrong move at the wrong time, and they'll dance t' my tune soon as this fracas is over. Let's get movin'."

Obediah Jones leaned across the horn of his saddle from behind a small stand of Quaking Aspen and surveyed what was left of Camp Winfield. Nothing remained standing, and elements of the Fifth Infantry were forming up, at the loud and insistent commands of officers and cadre, to follow the long line of wagons and troops that were slowly disappearing along a rutted trail into the wilderness along Ham's Fork of the Green River. All that remained as the large clearing emptied was a badly scarred and trampled meadow.

Lightly spurring his horse, Obediah moved from his place of concealment and trotted across the torn, half-frozen ground toward the last elements of the army that drained from the field like water from a broken dam.

"Well...is it me eyes that'r deceivin' me, now?" Sergeant Major O'Riley said, as he appeared from behind a retreating supply wagon. Reining up next to Obediah, he said, "An' here we was thinkin' you was dead, fer sure."

"O'Riley...what's this all about?" Obediah asked, waving his hand in the direction of the disappearing column.

"Well, now, lad," O'Riley said, a huge grin splitting his ruddy face, "what it's about is findin' someplace we can survive the winter. An' what else would ya suppose?"

Obediah scratched the stubble on his chin. "So, you're going to survive it all strung out in a line, rather than in camp?"

"Now...lad, don't be startin' with me as soon as ya get here," O'Riley said, the first signs of Irish irritation creasing his face. "When the Colonel needed ya, where was you? Nowhere t' be found that's where. There's times when things got t' be done, with or without ya."

"O'Riley...I don't mean any offense," Obediah said, nudging his horse up the now mucky trail, but I really don't think the Mormons need to worry about you and Alexander's army. You're all going to die of stupidity before they can get a good shot off in your direction."

"Is 'at so, is it?" the big Sergeant huffed, as he urged his horse after the scout.

"Uh-huh. Feel how warm it's gotten over night, and look at what's left of your trail."

"Well...what of it, man?"

"Well, out in this country, it's the thaw that precedes a storm. I'll bet your next month's pay that within three days this whole column is bogged down in three feet of snow and freezing to death in a blizzard worse than the last one and with nowhere to go."

"Is that a fact, now?" the Sergeant huffed incredulously.

"Where's Alexander? This stupidity has got to be stopped."

"Stupidity is it, now. Well, you just be tellin' that t' him."

"Let me guess. He's at the head of this column, right?"

"That he is. He left early this mornin' with the Tenth Infantry in the van, an' him sittin' ramrod straight at the head, like the true leader he is."

"Why didn't I guess as much?" Obediah asked, sarcastically.

For the better part of an hour, the two men rode in stubborn silence, passing the long, strung-out column of mounted soldiers, each trooper slumped in his heavy coat.

Finally in exasperation, Obediah asked, "Just how long do you suppose this column is, Sergeant?"

The big Irishman scratched his two-day growth of beard and squinted in concentration. "With careful thought and figgerin', we calculated it 'd be somethin like five'r six miles long—once we was on the march, that is t' say."

"Five or six miles long?" Obediah asked, in disbelief.

"Give'r take a couple," the Sergeant replied, off-handedly.

"Give'r take a couple," Obediah repeated slowly, shaking his head. "Give'r take a couple."

"Kind of reminds ya of the Exodus, don't it?" O'Riley said, turning in his saddle. "The one in the Bible, I mean?"

"I know the one you mean, O'Riley, and it kind of does," Obediah said. "And something like forty years of misery might just go along with it, if not something much worse."

"An' jest whaddaya mean by that, now?" O'Riley asked, his voice betraying his rising temper.

"Well, now, Sergeant Major O'Riley, just look around you and above you. I'll sell the pig and give you the farm, if you all don't freeze stiffer than a poker, right in your saddles, stuck in the mud, within three days."

"Issat so?"

"It is," Obediah said, spurring his horse to a faster pace. "That's not your biggest problem though, my Biblical friend."

"An' just what might that be?" O'Riley shouted, as he

kicked the sides of his horse in an effort to catch up, lest he lose this argument by simply not being present.

"Your biggest problems is, Alexander ain't no Moses," Obediah shouted over his shoulder.

"Well, now...just you wait a...."

"Nope...Moses would have chosen a desert. Our brave Colonel Alexander has chosen a mountain icebox filled with a good many enemies who are determined to keep him in the wilderness 'till he and all of the rest of you freeze."

From the ridge line on the west side of the Ham's Fork river the endless column could be seen snaking slowly through the trees and brush that lined the opposite bank below. The head of the column was no longer visible even from this vantage point, having passed hours ago. Nor could the end of the column that had cleared the Camp Winfield site early that morning be seen. It was a monotonous parade of horses and men interspersed among wagons and cannon, their breath visible in the frigid air as they trudged on in an unbroken procession of misery.

Benko Tatum closed his small telescope with a metallic snap, stuffed it into an inside pocket, and turned in his saddle toward the two men behind him. "Them fools's strung out like a big, half-froze snake," he said to no one in particular. "Talk about dumb. Strung out like that, them Mormon's could eat 'em fer lunch."

"Mormons ain't gonna do it, Benko," Teeter said.

"Whaddaya mean they ain't gonna do nothin'?" Benko snapped. "They been burnin' wagons and runnin' off their cattle an' such."

"Yeah," Teeter responded slowly, his breath puffing

white with each careful word, "but they ain't shot nobody. They ain't even acted like they was goin' t' shoot anybody, least ways 'till them troopers start down Echo Canyon—which it looks like now they ain't gonna do."

"Ma'be we oughta jest let 'em freeze, Benko," Jenks offered. "It's fixin' t' snow sure as shootin', an' it don't look like they got no forage fer them animals, an...."

"He's right Benko," Teeter said, sensing Benko's rising irritation. "They probably don't have much grub for themselves, for the matter of that. Leave 'em t' freeze, and let's get outta here."

"We ain't gonna let 'em freeze," Tatum said, with a snarl, "an' I'm about tired t' death with arguin' about it. That's too easy. I'm gonna start this fracas and put some galena in a few of them fools fer the Mormons jest like we been plannin', and we're gonna leave ol' Pughsey's hat, here, where they'll be sure t' find it.?"

"Where'd ya find that ol' beaver's hat?" Jenks asked, sensing the futility of any further argument.

"Right where he landed when I knocked 'im off'n his horse," Tatum shot back.

Teeter eyed his boss carefully. It was just like Tatum to take all the credit to himself. "Well, there's somethin' else we oughta be considerin', Benko."

Tatum reined his horse around to face his two companions, and slipped his right hand inside his heavy coat. The big Colt felt warm, hanging next to his leg. "An' what might that be, Teeter?" he said, his voice growing even uglier.

"Them soldier boys might just react mighty strongly," Teeter said, not missing the implied threat in Tatum's movement. "There's a lot of 'em down there, and they might just come right after whoever takes a shot at 'em. They got their backs t' the wall, an' every man among 'em knows it. Have ya thought about that, Benko?"

Benko Tatum slipped the thong off of the big Colt's hammer and pulled it loose in its holster. He had about gotten his craw full of all the foot-dragging, and the temptation to blow at least one argument out of the saddle was almost more than he could withstand. If it wasn't Teeter, it was Jenks or one of the others. Always arguing for a way out; never enough gumption to start something or, even better, end something. He could put Jasper Pughsey under and not even aim in his direction. These pony soldiers would see to it for him. And, given all of the difficulties they faced, they would probably make it a slow, proper hanging, and Benko Tatum intended to be there to see it. Nobody was going to get in his way.

"Don't try it Benko," Teeter said, staring at the spot where Benko's arm disappeared into his coat. "We're in this with ya. You don't need t' get all riled up. Besides, one shot now would put an end t' your scheme real fast."

Benko eyed the other two, looking for any sign of rebellion. He could probably drop both of them before they got their weapons out, but this kind of a show-down now would bring them soldier boys up here fast. This score could be settled after Jasper Pughsey's bacon was fried. "Then all we gotta do," he said, bringing his hand out in the open and resting it on his saddle horn, "is find the right spot, put a volley into that line, drop this hat, an' light a shuck outta here. There'll be so much confusion, it'll take 'em five minutes t' figger out what happened. By then we...."

"Yeah," Jenks said, "first thing they'll do is hit the ground an' wait t' be sure they ain't gonna get shot up even more."

"Jenks's got the idea," Tatum said, barely concealing the surprise in his voice. Jenks seldom caught on to anything, at least without a prolonged explanation. "By the time they figger they ain't gonna catch no more, we'll be long gone."

Teeter drew a deep breath and relaxed in the saddle studying Tatum's face. Why he had hung around with this snake all of these years was a wonder to him. Everything they did usually ended in some sort of disaster, and Tatum was so bent on putting an end to Jasper Pughsey, he could allow for nothing else. "Best we get on with it, then," he said, his voice low with resignation.

"I figger these coons's headed fer Sublette's Cutoff," Tatum said, nodding his head in the direction the army column was heading. "I know jest the spot fer startin' the party."

"I know where ya mean," Jenks said. "Jest where the Cutoff crosses Ham's Fork, huh."

"Jenks, sometimes you amaze me," Teeter said, making little effort to hide his disgust.

"Let's go then," Tatum said. "We've got a piece t' travel if we're gonna get there in time t' do it right."

CHAPTER THIRTEEN

Through the grey, swirling coldness of the intense blizzard, Benko Tatum, Will Teeter, and Jenks could see the forward elements of the long column threading diagonally through the small valley and crossing the shallow creek not more than a half a mile away. The three lay concealed in a shallow depression among the trees some eighty or ninety yards up the steep hillside. Alexander and his column would pass directly below them.

"It's gonna be like a turkey shoot," Tatum exclaimed. "Gimme Pughsey's hat," he said turning to Teeter lying in the snow next to him. "It ain't gonna be but another few minutes and the fur's gonna start flyin'. I want 'em t' find it jest as soon as they screw up enough gumption t' stick their heads up an' come up an' see who's done 'em in. "

"How do ya plan on doin' it, Benko?" Teeter asked.

"Whaddaya mean, how we gonna do it?" Tatum shot back. "All three of us are gonna open up on 'em as soon as they get in front of us. That's how we're gonna do it."

"But Benko," Jenks hissed from the other side of Teeter, "them what we're shootin' at 's gonna hit the dirt, but what about all a them pony soldiers lined up behind 'em far as we can see?"

Teeter looked with some surprise at the outlaw laying in the snow next to him. He had not thought of the reaction of the others either, and it astonished him to no end that Jenks had hit upon something so obvious when he had not. "Damnation...Jenks's got a point, Benko," he said, looking at the gang leader laying next to him. "What about the rest of 'em?"

"Well, what about 'em?" Benko shot back. "Jenks you keep that flap-jaw of yours shut, you dumb coon. You hear me? Thems what ain't shot through's gonna hit the dirt. I'm tellin' ya, ain't a man among 'em within ear-shot what's gonna stick his head up 'till he's good an' sure he ain't gonna get it blowed off. Besides, they been marchin' in this cold fer three long days," Benko Tatum snickered. "Why, them boys is so froze and miserable, it might not even dawn on 'em what's happenin', as any fool can plain see.

"But Benko," Teeter began, "maybe they...."

"Ma'be nothin'. I don't wanna hear no more. We came t' do it, and by the Eternal, we're gonna do it. Now, shut up, the both a ya!"

Jenks started to rise, but his legs, stiff from the cold caused him to lose balance.

"Whaddaya think yer doin', Jenks?" Teeter snapped, as Jenks fell against him.

"I ain't stayin' t' be a part a this," he said, struggling to find a foot hold in the snow. "It's crazy. All is gonna happen is we're gonna get ourselves killed, fer sure."

Benko rolled away from his two companions and brought his big Colt to bear on both of them. "Ain't a man among us what's goin' nowheres 'till this deed's done. Now," he said, cocking the hammer of the deadly weapon, "either you're gonna die facin' me right now, or you're gonna open up on them an' ma'be live t' tell about it."

"Don't point that thing at me," Teeter said, flattening out in the snow and leaving Jenks the sole target of Benko Tatum's hate. "I ain't leavin' 'till the confusion starts, just like we planned."

Staring down the huge black hole of the revolver's barrel, Jenks said, "I ain't neither...I reckon, Benko. Count me in," he said, slumping back into the cold concealment of the deepening snow. "Count me in," he sighed, with resignation. Besides, the way it's startin' t' snow, ain't likely they'll see us anyways."

Colonel Alexander slowly lifted his arm signalling the column to a halt. The snow that had been falling lightly most of the morning had in the past couple of hours steadily increased in intensity. A driving wind out of the north blew with such a cold, steady force that it obscured everything beyond a few yards in a howling rage of grey and white, and the temperature had dropped well below zero the night before. The struggling procession of weary, half-frozen men and animals came slowly to a halt as the Colonel's order passed on down the line to the Fifth Infantry troops at the rear of the column now seven miles long.

Turning to one of the men behind him in an effort to be heard above the howling wind, the Colonel shouted, "Corporal, ride back and find Sergeant O'Riley. Have him report to me, and be quick about it."

As Alexander watched the man turn and spur his reluctant horse toward the rear, the form of Obediah Jones emerged from the shroud of swirling white. "Jones...I think we'd better camp here. What do you think?"

"Colonel...animals are dropping in their tracks back there. Without forage, there's no way they can withstand this cold. A good number of your men are on foot now, as it is. They've just abandoned their horses where they dropped, equipment and all. You're going to lose half your cattle and horses before this thing's over. Men, too, if something isn't done fast.

"This storm will pass. All we need is a few more days," Alexander said, struggling to be heard over the howling wind.

"It's not going to pass," Obediah hollered back. "I've seen storms like this last for days in this country. By this time tomorrow, unless I miss my guess, it'll drop to thirty or forty below."

The two men sat facing each other slumped in silence, the blizzard covering their heavy coats and their horses with a freezing blanket of white. Each knew with a certainty bordering on desolation that what the Mormons had started, the mountains were now finishing.

Colonel Edmond Brooke Alexander slumped even deeper in his heavy coat. He could suddenly see his otherwise brilliant military career crashing down around him—ending, defeated by a blizzard in a campaign for which he was not fully responsible. His entire career, almost thirty-five years of hard work, was collapsing in these miserable, desolate, frozen mountains. "I've failed, Jones," Alexander said, his voice so low with resignation that Obediah could not hear him without leaning closer.

"What's that, Colonel?"

"I said...I've failed in my mission, Mr. Jones. They've won. Brigham Young and his fanatics have defeated me."

Anger welled up in Obediah Jones as he sat staring at the man who had time and again refused to listen to his counsel. All of this misery could have been avoided any number of times with the application of a minimum of common sense. Too few of the men arrogant enough to be making momentous decisions about the Mormons—a people about whom they knew virtually nothing—had the experience to make the kinds of judgments that had brought things to this sorry pass, and that was true of the whole chain of command, from Buchanan to Alexander. The hard truth was, none of it should have happened to begin with. It was not the Mormons or the mountains or the weather that had defeated the unfortunate man slumped in the snow before him. It was arrogance, stupidity, bigotry, and who knows what else? Obediah Jones knew the whole operation did not fail here in the cold, not just here in the mountains, but in Washington and wherever men were motivated by ignorance, venality, and hatred. That was what brought this commander and his pathetic army to such a wretched end. And the bitter truth was, as Obediah knew full well, it was not over yet—at least not for these unfortunate, half-frozen, would-be warriors, sent into this wilderness to pursue a petty national policy of intolerance.

"Well...Colonel, you...."

"O'Riley. Where's your mount?" Alexander shouted past Obediah.

"Give out, Colonel. Give out. He just laid down and quit a mile or so back, he did," O'Riley said, his breath coming in short, painful bursts. "And none of the men are in much better shape, sir, if I do say so meself, sir."

"Colonel," Obediah said, leaning toward the commander, "best we make camp while what's left of your command has the strength. There'll be plenty of time for self-recrimination later. The worst is yet to come, and we need to get prepared—pronto."

Turning to several officers who had moved forward when the column had stopped, Alexander shouted, "Get these men into bivouac and have all of the animals sheltered as well as possible. Pass the word on back."

Once again assuming command of a difficult situation,

the Colonel seemed to come alive. And renewed action seemed to instill a sense of hope within him and within those looking to him for leadership. "Take a horse from one of the enlisted men, and see to it, Sergeant Major."

As life began to return to the paralyzed column, Obediah swung his horse around and quickly disappeared into the blizzard as he made his way back down the line.

Benko Tatum could not believe his eyes. The whole column had come to a stop barely within range, but the intensity of the blizzard made it nearly impossible to distinguish the movements of the men at the van. They had waited, half-frozen, as the storm had increased in intensity, and now, just beyond reach, their quarry had come to a stop. "What're they doin'?" he hissed at Teeter.

Brushing the persistent snow from his eyes, Teeter said, "Seems like this fool blizzard finally stopped 'em."

"Looks t' me like they's about froze t' death, as it is, Benko," Jenks offered, in an effort to forestall the inevitable. "Ma'be we ain't gonna have t' put lead int' 'em."

Ignoring Jenks' irritating remarks, Benko Tatum lifted his big Hawken to his shoulder. "That looks like Alexander and Jones right at the head," he said, squinting down the long barrel. "I figger, from this distance, I can put that brass Colonel right outta his saddle fer good." Lifting his cheek from the stock of the Hawken, he turned to the other two, and said, "Teeter, you put lead into Jones, and Jenks you shoot the first one a them coons what looks this way."

Now that the time had come, Will Teeter felt a certain excitement, despite the danger involved in the ambush. "My pleasure," he said, slowly shoving his rifle through the snow and tucking it back against his shoulder. "Puttin' Jones under's gonna feel mighty fine." Benko was not going to give up, and it was too late now, anyway.

Turning back to the big rifle at his shoulder, Tatum said, "This Mormon war starts right about now, and it ain't too late. We dumped that coon Pughsey at about this distance," he chuckled. "Least ways he's gone under. Shot right through the lights, too. Jest like Alexander's gonna be."

"Yep...he is," Teeter agreed.

As Benko Tatum turned and started lining up his shot, Jenks slowly began to back away unnoticed by the other two. Somebody was going to get it in the lights alright, and Jenks was determined that it wasn't going to be him—or Alexander, for the matter of that. He had nothing against Alexander or Jones, and he was not going to get himself killed over another one of Benko Tatum's stupid notions.

As the other two talked, Jenks slid behind the bole of a huge pine and struggled to his feet, his frozen joints stubbornly refusing to hold his full weight as he leaned against the big tree. Now was the time to settle accounts with Benko Tatum—and with Will Teeter, too, if it came to that. Jenks knew he could surprise them both, and that would be enough.

Tatum and Will Teeter whirled around in the snow at the sound of Jenks' hammer snapping back, and both looked down the black throat of death as the muzzle of Jenks' Hawken traced small circles in the blowing snow, wavering uncertainly between the two of them.

"I ain't got nothin' again' you, Will Teeter, but you can make your play. It's Benko Tatum what's come t' the end of 'is trail. It's his blood what's gonna turn the snow red here abouts, an' nobody else's. An' no matter what you try, Teeter, I'll watch that coon bleed t' death if I hafta do it with my dying breath."

"Jenks," Tatum snarled, "you dumb coon, you...."

"Shut yer miserable mouth, Tatum," Jenks yelled, his voice shrill with years of pent-up frustration and hatred. "You called me a coon fer the last time. I've had all I can take of your ways, and I jest been waitin' fer the time I could put you under."

Slowly Will Teeter began sliding away from Benko. If he could get a shot off at Jenks, fine, but he didn't want any ball intended for Tatum to hit him by mistake.

"You can't get us both," Tatum spat.

"I ain't interested in you both," Jenks shot back. "Stay put Will, it's only Tatum what's gonna die t'day," he said, starting to squeeze the trigger.

The metalic snap from the trees behind him caused the surprised Jenks to pause a second too long.

The volley of shots that thumped through the trees on the near-by hillside, though muffled by the snow and wind, sounded near enough to the men at the head of Alexander's column to send even the most frozen trooper off his horse into the deep snow. In such a situation, no matter how cold, a man could not get close enough to the ground, but every mother's son within earshot got as flat as humanly possible.

Responding to the unexpected shots with the unequivocal smartness of a highly-trained soldier, Colonel Alexander yanked his horse's bridle viciously jerking its head sharply around to the left, and jumped to the ground pulling the animal down in the snow as a living revetment between him and the source of the gunfire.

Captain Jesse Gove plowed into the snow next to him, and threw a rifle across the horse's quivering flank. "Those damnable Mormons picked a fine time to ambush us, Colonel."

"...couldn't have picked a worse time, Captain," Alexander said, cautiously peering over his prostrate horse into the driving snow.

"Any idea how many or where they are?"

"I think up on the hillside, there. In this storm, who can tell? Could be a few or a whole division, I don't know," Alexander said, glancing around. "Was anyone hit?"

"I don't think so, sir. In all of this confusion, it's hard to tell. They hit us just as we were breaking up to establish camp. Could be just the usual harassment," Gove said, with more optimism in his voice than he felt.

"Let's hope so, Captain. But assuming this is something more serious, round up some troopers and see if you can't get a skirmish line spread out behind that embankment over on the right, and better be quick about it. If they come at us, we need to put up some sort of defense until we can get organized."

As Gove disappeared, Sergeant O'Riley scuttled through the deepening snow. "Things're startin' t' get organized back further, Colonel, but...word's spreadin' that there's trouble up here, sir," he said, trying to catch his breath. "Excuse me...sir, but crawlin' through this snow ain't the easiest thing...sir."

"Send a runner down the line through the Fifth Infantry and tell everyone to dig in until we find out what this is all about, and everybody else stay alert," Alexander said. "Get back here as quickly as you can."

Within minutes O'Riley had returned, with Gove and a dozen men crawling through the snow close behind him. Seeing the men, Alexander said, "Captain Gove, set up some sort of perimeter along that embankment," he said, gesturing off along the trail they had been following, "and string the men out back to this point. Things are quiet, I don't think we are going to get rushed. They'd have done it by now, probably."

"Likely they'll wait 'til dark, now," Gove offered, as he turned toward the men behind him.

"And have one of the men strip the gear off this horse when it's safe. Looks as if it's dead." Brushing the snow from the cold animal's neck, he gave it an affectionate pat. "...best horse I can remember having." With a sigh born of regret, he turned and said, "Come on Sergeant, let's see if we can check things out."

As the two crawled off through the snow, Gove could be heard deploying his men, his voice trailing off in the dense, blowing snow.

Jenks lay sprawled in the snow, the cold, powdery whiteness beneath him turning a bright crimson as his life slowly drained from his stiffening body. The ball from Benko Tatum's big Hawken had hit him squarely in the belly, violently throwing him back into Jasper Pughsey. It was the only thing that saved Jasper.

With the unmistakable sound behind him, Jenks had frozen, his attention fatally distracted. It was enough for Benko Tatum who jerked his weapon up and fired from the hip with deadly accuracy. As Jenks' body flew backward from the force of the ball, his rifle discharged, the shot grazing the side of Tatum's head, knocking him cold in the snow. Reacting to the unexpected action, Teeter twisted and jerked off a wild shot in the direction of the unknown intruder. The ball passed a few inches from Jasper's head as Jenks smashed into him knocking him backward into the snow-covered brush.

Teeter was straining to reload as Jasper Pughsey struggled to his feet, a crimson stain spreading down the side of his coarse, wool shirt. "Ain't no point in my killin' you, Will Teeter," he said, lifting the big Hawken. "Mine's the onlyest one what ain't gone off, but I can fix thet if I gotta."

Teeter lowered his weapon, and watched with astonishment as Jasper Pughsey toppled over in the snow. "Ain't no point in us killin' each other, we...." he said, his voice trailing of. There was no need for him to finish. There seemed to be no one left to hear him, until he felt the cold muzzle of Colonel Edmond Alexander's revolver press into his neck at the base of his skull.

"Don't move a muscle, mister, or you'll...."

"Holy Mother of...look what you've done, lad," Sergeant O'Riley said, as he pushed past Alexander. Yanking Teeter's rifle out of his hands, the big Irishman knelt in the snow and bent to examine Benko Tatum more closely.

"I didn't do none of this, I only got off one...."

"Tatum ain't dead, sir. Looks like he's only out cold for a while, if I do say so meself, sir."

Grabbing Teeter by the shoulder, Colonel Alexander yanked him to his feet, and pushed the barrel of his revolver deep into the man's belly. "The only thing I want to hear from you is where the rest of your murdering pack of

Mormons is hiding, and I'm in no mood to listen to any of your lies," he said, shoving Teeter backward into the snow. "Start talking, mister."

"His name's Will Teeter, and he isn't any Mormon, Colonel."

Alexander twisted around at the unexpected sound of Obediah Jones' voice, his attention momentarily drawn from the prostrate Teeter.

Despite the cold and the aching in his half-frozen body, Teeter rolled behind Alexander, and with surprising quickness reached beneath O'Riley and yanked Tatum's big Colt from under his snow-covered coat, kicking Alexander's legs out from under him. Struggling to his feet and waving the big revolver a few inches from Sergeant Major O'Riley's surprised face, Teeter said, "Don't nobody move."

"Don't try it, Teeter," Obediah said, slowly lifting his Hawken in Teeter's direction. "One of us will put you down before you get more than a yard away."

"Then what we got us here, Jones, is a mountain man's stand-off, ain't it? Ain't just one gonna die here. No matter how it plays out, there's gonna be at least two."

"You can't do it, Teeter. Besides, those are U. S. Cavalry troopers trying to find their way up here. You don't have a chance."

"I'm warnin' ya," Teeter said, waving the revolver between the three men.

"Stop and think, man," Alexander said. "You'll not...."

"Then we gotta pow-wow—and fast, or I'll take at least two, and maybe all three, of ya with me."

"Will," Obediah said, calmly, "let's all back off a bit, and the Colonel, here, will have a tent set up. We can get these two some medical care, and see if we can't get this all sorted out. Colonel, if you'll...."

"I have no intention of wasting my time talking with this man, Jones," Alexander huffed. "Why...he's...."

Obediah's big Hawken moved ominously in the Colonel's direction. "Colonel your unwillingness to listen to anyone but yourself has gotten us all into this mess. Your men are strung out for seven miles in a killing blizzard, two men may bleed to death, a third is dead, and you're arguing about who you'll talk with. Seems more likely, you ought to be concerned about who you'll die with, if you don't exert some real leadership here."

Captain Gove and several men appeared through the storm, their chests heaving from the exertion of the climb through the deep snow. "I thought we'd never find you, sir. We heard your voices and...what's going on, sir?" he said, his voice suddenly tense with alarm.

"We're all coming down now, Captain," Alexander said, his voice somewhat subdued. "Will you and Sergeant O'Riley please see that some sort of camp is pitched. We need shelter quickly. And have some of the men get these two down the mountain so they can be looked after. I don't think there will be any more trouble—at least for the time being."

Two miserable weeks later, on November 2, 1857, with the snow still falling, a half-starved, thoroughly demoralized, and badly depleted army made a temporary camp at the confluence of two forks of the Green River a dozen miles or so northeast of what was left of Fort Bridger. They had gained nothing in their forced march, and now they were faced with the worst that a high mountain winter has to offer the arrogant and inexperienced: dangerously low supplies, dying animals with little forage, wagons and caissons with their wheels frozen to their axles, frost-bitten soldiers, and perilously frigid temperatures dropping lower every night.

Here it was that early one morning, a day or so later, a much relieved Colonel Edmond Brooke Alexander turned his temporary command over to Colonel Albert Sidney Johnston of the Second United States Cavalry, an experienced officer whose ability was questioned by no one.

"I apologize, sir, for the condition of this command," Alexander said. "Our efforts, if stymied by the Mormons, seem to have been defeated by this frigid environment."

"I have met with no more success," Colonel Johnston responded, understandingly. "I left Fort Leavenworth with nearly a hundred and fifty horses, and now I have no more than ten. It would seem that our efforts are brought to a virtual stand still. Do you have any suggestions, Colonel?"

"My one remaining scout tells me that our best chance for survival would be at Fort Bridger—or what's left of it."

"What do you mean, what's left of it?" Colonel Johnston said, looking up from his cluttered camp desk.

"Apparently the Mormons burned it days ago. But there are still walls standing, and between the surrounding forest and whatever is left at the fort, we should be able to construct sufficient shelter to make it through the winter."

Colonel Johnston pushed his chair back and walked to the flap of the small tent. "Then let's start right now. Before it's too late."

The straggling army that entered the ruins of Fort Bridger on the afternoon of November 18, 1857, could have waged battle against no one. To a man, they had been defeated, not by the dreaded Mormons, not even by the unfamiliar terrain and hostile weather conditions, but by the bigotry and arrogance of the government they served, and by their own vanity and stupidity.

EPILOGUE

"Doesn't look any more inviting than it did the last time I was here, Jasper," Obediah said.

"Nope...it's a plumb unwelcome sight fer someone what knows he ain't been invited."

The two mountain men sat at the eastern end of Echo Canyon, with a cold evening wind to their backs. The canyon sloped gently away from them into what became a gorge toward its rock-walled bottom several miles below.

"Yew figger them dumb coons'll make it into Great Salt Lake?" Jasper asked with a chuckle.

"Well...I suppose anyone determined enough can blast their way anywhere they want to go. But if you're asking me if I think Johnston's army is going to force its way through here, the answer is: not without a lot of bloodshed—or Brigham Young's blessing."

"Uh-huh...me, too," Jasper stretched and shifted his weight in his saddle, obviously favoring his slowly healing side.

"You hurtin', partner?"

"Not so's you'd notice," Jasper said, hiding his discomfort. "Out ridin' yew still ain't much of a problem fer this child, an' don't yew be fergetin' it, neither."

"Neither one of ya looks too harmful from here."

"What the...." Jasper hollered, as he and Obediah spun in their saddles to face Orrin Porter Rockwell.

"Damnation...thet hurts," Jasper said, holding his side.

"You ever think of knocking?" Obediah said, his voice betraying his irritation at being caught off guard. "I swear, even your horse is a sneak."

"Me an' him's just doin' our jobs," Rockwell said, ignoring the tone of Obediah's voice and giving his horse's neck an affectionate pat. "I was sittin' here mindin' my own business when you two rode up cluckin' like a couple of Sunday school girls. You recollect we're expectin' unwelcome visitors hereabouts?"

"Ain't nobody comin' this way," Jasper said. "Thet army you been expectin'll be lickin' its wounds 'till spring."

"I know that, and you two know that. I watched 'em when they finally arrived at Bridger. Thet so-called army wasn't none too pretty a sight, I'll tell ya. But them boys down yonder, they don't know that," Rockwell said, nodding his head toward the canyon. "They got itchy fingers, too. What with bein' away from their warm beds an' all."

"Those troopers'll be lucky if they don't all starve before this winter's out," Obediah observed.

"They ain't gonna starve," Rockwell said. "I'll sell m' hog and give ya m' farm if President Young don't send 'em some supplies when he hears what's happened. Let's get on down the canyon and have poor Brother Pughsey, here, looked after."

"Poor Brother...now, jest a...."

"Brother Pughsey?" Obediah said, turning to face his old friend. "Well, now...Brother Pughsey, you...."

"Jest hesh up," Jasper grumbled as the three turned and rode into the canyon. "The day's gonna come when...."

The room was crowded and hot, but the meeting had been too short for those privileged to be present. Every man in the room had played a vital role in bringing the conflict to a relatively peaceful conclusion. And, while no one was satisfied with, or felt that a truly peaceful and permanent conclusion had been reached, all were grateful that there had been no bloodshed—no soldier had fallen before hostile Mormon fire, no Latter-day Saint had died in protecting that which was precious to him.

When they finally entered the valley in the spring, the troops had found a somber city, one in which they were not welcome. They had moved through a city that had not, in any sense of the word, been conquered. The few Latter-day Saints that lined the dusty street that spiteful spring day had watched with defiance as the troopers under the newly-promoted General Johnston paraded through the nearly empty city and on toward the desert to the west. Nearly every home was empty, and the men that were left were there to put the torch to the city, if the army made so much as one hostile move. Nor would the Saints return, until their peace and safety was assured.

It was a peaceful conclusion to the conflict—the Utah War, as it came to be known—but one that gave little satisfaction to anyone and no sense of resolution.

"We met the challenge," President Young said. "We met it with strength, and we met it with honor. We met it with the righteous rigor that the Children of God of all ages have met such adversity. We met it as Moses met it; we met it as David met it; we met it as Nephi met it; we met it as Moroni met it; and we met it as Joseph always met it. And in the name of Israel's God, we will meet it again whenever the necessity arises."

From the back of the room, Jasper Pughsey, sitting next to Obediah Jones and Porter Rockwell, strained to read the title embossed on the spine of the large book the Prophet took from his desk. The volume was bound in rich leather and imprinted in gold letters, but Jasper was too far away to make out the title.

"What are you doing?" Obediah whispered.

"I'm tryin' t' make out the title of thet book."

"You mean to tell me you can't tell what that is?"

"Well now...if'n I could tell, I wouldn't be squintin' like this, would I, Mr. Smart...."

"It's the Bible, Jasper," Obediah whispered. "You always manage to pick the wrong ti...."

"Well...jest hesh yerself befer ya ruin everythin'."

As Brigham Young carefully, almost lovingly, turned the gilt-edged pages, he said, "As everyone here knows, these things are not new to human history. They have been predicted in holy scripture and in the writings of holy men throughout the ages."

He paused as his eyes scanned the page before him. "The course of events these past few months—not to mention the past years—has caused me to turn again to the Book of Revelation, always a somber contemplation. Somber because, as you know, John saw our day and the days that are to follow, and what he saw was not pleasant. In my reading the other night, I came across a particular passage that for some reason stood out for me."

The Prophet turned the page and his finger traced down the delicate paper and stopped. Clearing his throat, he said, "Forgive me of one quote before we leave what has happened here to future historians."

Fumbling with his glasses he paused and then read:

> And when the thousand years are expired, Satan shall be loosed out of his prison, And shall go out to deceive the

nations which are in the four quarters of the earth, Gog and Magog, to gather them together to battle: the number of whom is as the sand of the sea. And they went up on the breadth of the earth, and compassed the camp of the saints about, and the beloved city: and fire came down from God out of heaven, and devoured them.

Quietly closing the book, Brigham Young looked at the faces before him. With him at the front of the room were his two counselors and members of the Council of the Twelve. Daniel Wells, General of the successful Militia, sat on his right, and President Heber C. Kimball to his left.

"In our short history we have lost one beloved city, and we have lost a beloved prophet. Thanks to you here and many others, we have not yet lost this beloved city, this 'camp of the Saints'," he said, his hand sweeping toward the window and South Temple Street beyond. "The question on many lips of recent days," the Prophet said, his eyes searching the group before him, "has been whether it is over or whether we will continue to endure this kind of thing in the future? The scriptures are open to all and speak eloquently of our times and of the future. While the Apocalypse speaks of yet a future time, a millennial time perhaps not too distant in the future, these past few months have a certain similarity to that of John's disquieting vision of the final conflict," the Prophet said, holding the Bible up for all to see.

"Satan is undoubtedly loose among the nations of the earth, and has been from the Fall. He knows the minds of men in our own time—but more importantly, in our own nation. And at times our enemies have seemed to be as numberless as the sands of the sea. That was true in Missouri and it was true in Illinois. And, like Nauvoo just a decade ago, this beloved city—our 'camp of the Saints', our refuge in the tops of the mountains—was indeed unrighteously set upon. But throughout this past winter, it must have seemed to our enemies that it was they who were about to be devoured—if not by fire, at least by snow and ice."

A wave of subdued laughter rippled through the room and a few voiced their agreement with murmurs of "amen." The sound of voices and a relaxed shuffling of feet filled the room as the Prophet set the book down on his desk.

"While our people are returning to their homes, it is not over. I need not remind you that encamped to the west of us is an army that will continue to remain a threat. While I urge every Latter-day Saint to give allegiance to Governor Cumming and his administration, I also urge vigilance. None is to be trusted."

Looking up, the Prophet saw Jasper Pughsey and Obediah Jones sitting with Lot Smith and Porter Rockwell, the four almost lost at the rear of the room.

"Brethren," the Prophet said, quieting the room once again. "Words cannot express my thanks to all of you. But there have been a few who have gone the extra mile in our behalf, not the least of whom is Colonel Thomas L. Kane. I wish he could be with us here today, but as many of you know he has returned to his home in the east in very poor health.

"He arrived here last February in the midst of cold and snow and war, after a harrowing trip via the Isthmus of Panama and across the desert—an unofficial emissary of the President of the United States—in an effort to bring the conflict to a peaceful conclusion. Many fruits were born of his efforts. Thanks to him, Governor Cumming entered our valley peacefully and now presides as the chief executive officer of the territory—to no small degree, a consequence of Brother Kane's selfless efforts.

"Before he left, I told Brother Kane, as I am telling you now, that the Lord sent him here, and that the Lord would not take him from this earth until his work is done. I told him that I wanted him to live with the Saints to all eternity, and I meant every word of it. He has done a great work.

"And there have been others among us who, though not ordinarily part of our number, must also be thanked— especially one whose sacrifice went far beyond that of a mere friend. I shall take care of that myself in a moment," he said, his glance returning to Jasper.

The Prophet scanned the crowded room, and said, "Now, we must return to our families and our flocks. We must return to our homes confident in the Lord's continued blessings. But remain vigilant, brethren. Remain vigilant."

Turning to his First Counselor in the First Presidency, Brigham Young said, "President Kimball, will you bring this meeting to a close, please?"

Jasper Pughsey and Obediah Jones shuffled toward the door as everyone jostled to leave the over-crowded room.

"Well...thet was one of the derndest things I ever heard," Jasper said.

"Why's that, Jasper?" Obediah responded, sensing an opportunity to needle his old friend.

"I never knowed them words was in the Bible. Did you, Obediah?"

"What do you know about what's in the Bible? An old hoss like you'd...."

"Well...thet ain't the point, Mr. Smart...."

"Brother Pughsey," Brigham Young called from the front of the noisy room. "May I see you alone for a moment, please."

Startled, the old mountain man turned and saw the Mormon Prophet motioning to him.

"What've you done now, *Brother* Pughsey? Looks like I might have to break you out of the hoosegow again," Obediah chuckled, giving his partner a shove toward the front of the room. "I'll be waiting outside—*Brother* Pughsey."

As Jasper approached, the Prophet took his hand and shook it warmly. "How do we ever thank you for the sacrifices you have made in our behalf?" he asked, putting his arm around Jasper's shoulder. "I'm told that you are healing, as you should, now you've got a warm bed and plenty of food."

"Well, now...I...it...."

General Wells stood nearby. "He went more than the extra mile for us, President Young. His help was invaluable, and it nearly cost him his life—more than once, I might add."

"Indeed," the Mormon Prophet said, taking Jasper by the elbow. "Come with me, Brother Pughsey. There's something I would like to show you."

With some confusion, Jasper Pughsey followed Brigham Young down a dark, cool hallway and out into the blinding sunlight of a warm, late spring day in the tops of the mountains. The Prophet led him across the yard to a corral, and stepping through a narrow gate, the two crossed to an enclosed stable.

As Jasper's eyes slowly adjusted, the darkness seemed to melt away, and the old mountain man saw standing in the back of the stable the most magnificent white gelding he had ever seen.

The large animal's magnificent head came up, and his ears pricked forward as the two men slowly approached. The Prophet produced a large green apple from somewhere, and the horse nickered and cautiously stepped toward them.

To Jasper, the animal had an almost startling look of intelligence in its large, brown eyes.

"His name is Major," Brigham Young said quietly, as the animal took the apple from his hand. "I gave him that name the first time I laid eyes on him," he said. "It was the name of Joseph's horse, and no two animals could look or act more alike."

For some reason Jasper Pughsey could not explain, tears welled up in his eyes and slowly trickled down his leathery cheeks.

"What he represents," the Prophet said, rubbing the horse's velvety nose and stroking its heavily muscled neck, "is the finest: the purity of unblemished white—decency, integrity, goodness, and a pristine independence of spirit. A kind of wildness that only the unrighteous hand of man can destroy, yet requires understanding and constant, loving attention if it is to be maintained as God intended."

The big horse nickered and his skin quivered where Jasper gently laid his hand.

"That is something I think you understand, Jasper Pughsey," the Prophet said. "There's much of the same in you. That's why this animal could belong to no one else."

"To...you mean...I...."

"It's a kind of righteous wildness, isn't it?" the Prophet asked, ignoring the mountain man's confusion. "A refusal to submit, to be broken by the world. A refusal to bend to man's foolish demands."

Jasper Pughsey looked at the Mormon Prophet, and found himself almost unable to speak. "How...how'd you know?"

"I think it's the kind of thing shared by men who love and treasure the right things for the right reasons, Brother Pughsey—men of all times and of all ages. Under the skin—down deep where it counts—they are brothers. And because they are, some things seldom need to be spoken. They are simply understood."

The large, white horse looked around at the mountain man and gently nudged his shoulder.

THE END